My Curious Uncle Dudley

MY Curious UNCLE DUDLEY

Barry Yourgrau

illustrated by Tony Auth

CANDLEWICK PRESS
CAMBRIDGE, MASSACHUSETTS

Text copyright © 2004 by Barry Yourgrau
Illustrations copyright © 2004 by Tony Auth

First edition 2004

Library of Congress Cataloging-in-Publication Data
Yourgrau, Barry.
My curious uncle Dudley / Barry Yourgrau ; illustrated by Tony Auth. — 1st ed.
p. cm.
Summary: While under the temporary care of his "curious and marvelous" uncle Dudley, eleven-year-old Duncan Peckle has a summer of adventures, which include magic spells, goblins, and bubble-riding.
ISBN 0-7636-1935-3
[1. Uncles—Fiction. 2. Magic—Fiction. 3. Humorous stories.] I. Auth, Tony, ill. II Title.
PZ7.Y8959My 2004
[Fic]—dc21   2002042882

2 4 6 8 10 9 7 5 3 1

Printed in the United States of America

This book was typeset in Centaur.
The illustrations were done in watercolor and ink.

Candlewick Press
2067 Massachusetts Avenue
Cambridge, Massachusetts 02140

visit us at www.candlewick.com

To Sarah and David,
niece and nephew

CHAPTER ONE
voyager in the guest room

My young life changed forever one July afternoon, with a knock on my bedroom door, and my father's head sticking in to announce, "Better go clean up what's yours in the guest room. Someone's going to be staying with us awhile!" His head disappeared as I groaned, "No, not Aunt Mac again." Thinking of my mother's crabby old aunt.

"Worse!" my father's voice cried from down the hall. "Your uncle Dudley, God in heaven help us!"

"God in heaven help us" was what my father said whenever something was just too much to bear.

My uncle Dudley got under my poor father's skin, you see. Because of his way of living, I guess. Although I suspect a certain amount of sibling jealousy, or whatever you call it, came into the picture. Being an only child myself, I can't say for sure about this. But I suspect.

Now, I'd only met my uncle Dudley once before, back when I was five. We were living in Marigold Falls then, before moving here to Mt. Geranium. We drove all the way to Boston, to see Uncle Dudley at the hotel where he was staying the night before "embarking on another great voyage!" That's how he talked. From that visit I remembered mainly that Uncle Dudley was very thin and had a stringy goatee beard. And he wore a Panama hat, even indoors, tilted back, and a dirty tweed jacket, with a hole in the sleeve, which was scratchy when he gave a shout and put his arms around me.

But particularly I recalled his hotel bed, because it had a purple blanket that I greatly enjoyed jumping up and down on, which Uncle

Dudley observed with a kindly gleam, while my father and mother kept asking me to kindly stop.

And now here he was, my uncle Dudley of the "great voyages," three months after my eleventh birthday, climbing out of our green family Dodge. My father had parked with his usual scrape-and-jolt along the hedge in the driveway. Our guest stopped and threw open his arms.

"By Jupiter and the seven planets!" he cried, getting the number wrong, like he often did, as I'd find out. "If it isn't my favorite nephew, Duncan!"

He looked just how I remembered, apart from sporting an alarmingly brown tan and being perhaps even bonier. His Panama hat was maybe a bit more battered—and his tweed jacket boasted a few more holes and was now far too short above the wrists. But he still had his stringy goatee. There was a patch missing from it now, as if someone or something had taken a bite.

My father struggled out between the car and the hedge, and we all dragged Uncle Dudley's banged-up blue suitcase out of the trunk, and up the back steps, where my mother was waiting.

My father was not in the greatest of moods.

Not just from scratching the car on the hedge again, or Uncle Dudley's arrival in general. But because Uncle Dudley had somehow gotten advance word of his visit to the *Geranium Gazette,* our fine local newspaper.

WORLD-FAMOUS AUTHOR COMES CALLING!

blared the headline on the front page. "Dudley Peckle, internationally famed scribe, pays heed to family ties!" the article announced, and then it named my father and mother, Professor and Mrs. Norris Peckle, and our address here on Clover Crescent.

Now, my father considered Uncle Dudley a showoff (true) and a boaster (also true: Uncle Dudley's claim to "world fame" was exactly one very small, mysterious book he had published only in Japan; the original English manuscript had been "lost overboard somewhere on the high seas". . . supposedly).

But really I think my father just hated to see our family name made so public.

Peckle: It's not a name with which you get along easily in the world! Imagine a whole classroom reciting, "Peter picked a peck of pickled peppers . . ." and then looking around to screech with laughter at you, and you'll have some idea. I know my father once considered shortening our last name by a couple of crucial letters. In the end he took the courageous path and stuck with Peckle, though he made a point of keeping its six letters out of the spotlight.

Now here came Uncle Dudley flaunting it for all of Mt. Geranium to gawk at! "God in heaven help us!"—I heard a lot of that phrase those days.

And so Uncle Dudley moved into the guest room on the third floor, at the top of the stairs near the attic. He was here to "heed family ties." And to "bone up on some researches," whatever that meant. Nobody was quite sure what, exactly, he did. Had we known, my father would have chased Uncle Dudley back out the driveway, that's for certain. And all the way out of town.

But at the time, as I say, none of us had a clue.

❖ ❖ ❖

After a week or so, here's what I *had* learned about our visitor:

—He was a bachelor, never married; but there had once been "a great love . . . a great love!" in his life.

At the thought of which Uncle Dudley would touch his sleeve, over the spot where a faint tattoo of a broken heart marked his arm (a tattoo!). And pull at his mothy goatee in misty silence.

—He ate like a horse (as my father grumbled), yet somehow stayed thin as a stick.

"What marvel of *l'art culinaire* is this?" he would cry at dinnertime, holding out his plate for thirds, while the rest of us were barely through openers. "'Regular old meatloaf,' you call it? Nonsense!" he would sneer. "*Impossible!* More mashed potatoes, please!"

Not that Uncle Dudley ever bought any groceries (as my father grumbled some more). That wasn't his style. What he did was bring flowers to my mother—a red, yellow, and green bouquet every couple days, droopy, and not exactly fresh, but wrapped in fancy crinkly tissue paper, from the florist in town center. And my

mother would blush and shake her head at the fancy attention.

—Uncle Dudley slept late. *Very* late.

Bright and early weekday mornings, my father scraped the green Dodge out the driveway and stopped-and-started off toward the campus of Geranium College for Girls, where he was a dean, a sort of assistant principal. My mother put in a load of laundry or weeded in one of her flower beds, and then had her half-day volunteering at Florence Nightingale Hospital.

My school was over for the summer. So there was just me, it turned out, to greet our curious guest each day as he came clomping downstairs, at last, in his stained and faded satin bathrobe (everything Uncle Dudley wore was stained and faded) and floppy, tattered brown pointed shoes.

And I felt a curious deep thrill, as if a character had stepped right out of the dusty pages of *A Thousand and One Arabian Nights*—to sit at our kitchen table, slurping instant coffee in the midday sunshine.

"So, Favorite Nephew!" this character would announce, with a wink from under his Panama hat. "How fair blows the wind o' this bright balmy morn!"

Not that Uncle Dudley talked in this old-time storybook way all the time. Just most of it. Enough to make my father mutter, "God and *such*, Dudley. Don't you ever do anything with your mouth like a normal person!" My father had a way of asking questions that really weren't.

"Not . . . if I can help it . . ." Uncle Dudley

replied, thinking over the topic surprisingly hard and long, before he turned my way and winked.

—Among the various "research materials" up in Uncle Dudley's room was a certain shrunken head from Mexico—

But I'm getting ahead of myself.

My shrunken-head discovery didn't come until Uncle Dudley and I were left alone in the house that summer. When my parents went to visit Aunt Mac in Ohio.

I sometimes wonder: What would have happened if Aunt Mac, whose real name is Hildegarde but whom we always call Mac, hadn't complained yet again in her whiny way about being lonely and forgotten? "She's surrounded by relatives," my father protested. "But you wouldn't know it to listen to her!"

"We really have to visit, I suppose," sighed my mother. "It's family duty. We've put it off for so long. But driving all that way just for a few days with Aunt Mac, it seems so . . ." My mother didn't say "dreary," but that's why she sighed again.

And then all at once a look came into her eyes. "Unless we took our time coming back," she declared. "Driving slowly, a scenic way? Just the two of us, Norris? Alone—for the first time in a long, long while?"

"Alone?" said my father. "But what about Duncan?"

"Dudley will look after Duncan," replied my mother. "They'll have a wonderful time." She smiled happily at me across the breakfast table.

I blinked back, thrilled at her inspiration.

"Oh, Norris, say yes?" said my mother.

"Dad?" I nodded, grinning enthusiastically.

"Dudley will look after Duncan . . . ?" repeated my father. Sounding not nearly so enthusiastic.

"What, act *in loco parentis* for Duncan? With pleasure!" declared Uncle Dudley, when the idea was brought up to him at supper. His fancy ancient Latin was his way of saying he'd be a substitute parent.

"And George Feeley, who lives down the block, will look in every once in a while. Just in case," added my father.

I'm sure my father emphasized plain old "just in case" to Mr. Feeley, who had been my Cub Scout leader.

◆ ◆ ◆

So barely a month after Uncle Dudley's arrival—
after my mother had stuffed the basement freezer
with enough TV dinners to open a supermarket,
and had run up the front steps a third time to kiss
me and make sure Uncle Dudley had all the right
phone numbers and addresses—the green Dodge
rolled and jerked away down the street, with my
father tooting the horn and my mother waving her
handkerchief, her arm jerking forward and back,
thanks to my father's driving. Until they were out
of sight.

And then it was just me and my curious and marvelous uncle Dudley.

I looked up at him shyly and he gave me a tap on the chin. And then he turned toward the screen door, rubbing his bony hands and contemplating with a smack of his lips the pleasures of deciding what to choose for dinner.

And Mt. Geranium's magical summer spread all around us.

I was spending a lot of my time at Gumberry Creek that summer. With my best friend, Arthur Shetlock, I had developed a scheme of diving for lost treasure—meaning the quarters and dimes

dropped from sloshing waders' pockets, plus anything else valuable or shiny that litterbugs might have dumped in. Arthur and I had formed our own company, Gumberry Salvage Corp. We operated an inner tube, painted with our company logo: a dolphin wearing a snorkel and proudly brandishing a hook.

During diving breaks now, I stirred Arthur's envy about my first evenings alone with Uncle Dudley. How, after dining on TV dinners, my *in loco parentis* and I would sit together out in the backyard in the lawn chairs, while he smoked his pipe (forbidden indoors by my mother) made of yellowing actual whalebone.

And how he'd send me in for the newspaper, from which he'd construct two big paper hats for us, which we then put on together, after he removed his Panama—for storytelling by moonlight! "Finest light in the world," said Uncle Dudley. "The old celestial bubble-lantern!" (Besides the moon, Uncle Dudley was just crazy about bubbles.) Tales of adventure and seafaring he'd tell, down there by the old Panama Canal, in the port of Valparaíso where the moon—

"Valparaíso's not in Panama," interrupted Arthur.

He was scowling in his soaked T-shirt, with our ballpointed logo bleeding on it.

"Whadda you mean?" I said.

"Valparaíso's in Chile," said Arthur. He was a geography fiend in social studies.

"But Uncle Dudley said Panama. By the Canal."

Arthur shook his head and blinked beneath the snorkeling mask up on his brow. Gumberry Creek dribbled from his nose.

"Chile," he said.

You know, I didn't even bother arguing. I just looked out at the waters of Gumberry, and shrugged a cool pitying shrug—just as Uncle Dudley might have, I thought. I knew how pitifully envious Arthur must be about my voyaging relative. After all, he'd been featured on the front page of the *Gumberry Gazette!*

The next day I got my glimpse of the shrunken head.

It was early afternoon. A package arrived for Uncle Dudley. A curious, slender package, excessively tied up with twine. I climbed with it to the third floor, gazing at the return address in peculiar green ink on the plain brown wrapper: KNICHTBUBEL INST. OF EAST BROOKLYN, NEW YORK. I knocked. I knocked again. After still another knock, I was told to enter.

I had not been inside the guest room since my uncle arrived. How so much stuff could have come out of one battered blue suitcase, I couldn't explain. But Uncle Dudley sat perched at the rickety card table by the window amidst a sea of papers and books—teetering sandcastles of papers and books!—and weird old leather cases, and strange old boxes, and very odd packets. All piled, stacked, and crammed every way. All littered with crumpled socks.

When he saw what I had in my hands, my uncle dropped his pencil and came leaping through the clutter to take it from me. His dressing gown flapped like buzzard wings under the dirty white of his Panama hat.

"At last!" he cried. "From the great Dr. Feathergold himself. The research I've been waiting for!"

To my young ignorant ears the name Feathergold meant nothing right then.

I was too busy staring at what sat on the plaid blanket of the guest-room pullout bed.

"Is that . . . a . . . *a shrunken head?*" I stammered.

"Eh?" muttered Uncle Dudley, staring himself at the bundle in his lap. Finally he looked up and took notice.

"Oh. Yes. Bartered for that grim beauty deep in the Mexican jungle. From the cannibals! Well, go on——" he said, waving me to take a closer look.

I inched forward through the piles, and stood carefully over the bed. The little dark face snarled up at me, its black shriveled lips twisted.

"Go on, go on," Uncle Dudley insisted, grinning as he sawed away at his package's twine with a dinner knife from the kitchen.

I reached down, hesitantly, and touched the dusty head of hair.

"It feels . . . *artificial!*" I exclaimed.

"Don't it!" Uncle Dudley agreed, delighted. "Hold it aloft there, nephew!"

After more hesitating, I lifted the gruesome thing into the air between two careful fingers. "'*Recuerdo de Mexico,*'" I read aloud haltingly from the little lettering under the tiny chin.

"Poor old Señor Recuerdo!" sighed Uncle Dudley. "Evil way to go. Evil, evil . . . But let us not brood, young Duncan," he cried, "on the ways of the jungle and its barbarities! Not when they're finally here: by the seven scribes of Baghdad, I mean *the precious pages of Feathergold!*"

And with this the twine snapped, and a new load of pages went slooshing off into the paper sea around us.

No, I did not comprehend the dire consequences of the package I had carried up to the third floor. On that summer afternoon, I was just a kid caught up in the shivery thrill of a shrunken head on a blanket, with its dark slits for eyes, its dusty creepy hair.

But I would comprehend, by the very next day.

CHAPTER TWO
a cry for help

Chocklee's Illustrated World Encyclopedia had been on sale once among the detergent and bird-food specials at Chocklee's Supermarket in town center. I owned—had purchased with my allowance—all three volumes. The encyclopedia's entries were scrawny and the print extra-large. But the illustrations were a treasure, all finely colored and labeled.

I was in my room next afternoon, consulting the entry on *Shrunken Heads.* I'd earlier checked the map of Chile, which perplexingly *did* include

Valparaíso, like Arthur said. Panama's little map, for some reason, did not.

But I found a terrific picture of a shrunken head—though from Africa, not Mexico. I was using this as a guide for my redesign of the Gumberry Salvage Corp. logo, which would now feature a shrunken head snarling on top of the dolphin's nose. I was working on a colored-pencil drawing, to impress and convince my partner, Arthur.

Outside, Clover Crescent lazed in the summer sunshine. I got so involved in my redesign that I was barely aware of the afternoon heat or the time passing. I can get that way.

Which is probably why it took me so long to hear the faint cry.

But then I stopped my aquamarine pencil. I looked out, then around. Then up.

The voice was coming from above. The floor above me.

"Help," it was repeating, very calmly—almost dignified. "I say, *help* . . ."

I peered out into the hall. "Uncle Dudley?" I called, hesitantly. Silence. Then again, faintly:

"*Help* . . . I say. *Help* . . ."

My heart began to beat fast. I went to the door to the third-floor stairs. I opened it. I heard the cries, more clearly.

"Uncle Dudley?" I called back. "Hello?"

Unsure, I started up. I'd never heard an adult calling for help before! I waited breathless outside the guest-room door. I called again. The cries repeated. I knocked. With a hammering heart, I turned the handle. I peered inside.

The shock I got was so, well, *shocking*, I don't remember if I was too paralyzed to scream, like in your worst nightmares, and only gasped.

But I recall for sure my hair stood on end.

There in the dim room on the dim plaid blanket, where yesterday one lonesome tiny head had sat, now sat a second. Regular size. Not a head exactly—a pair of shoulders, from which stuck a neck and a goateed mouth and a nose and cheeks and an ear.

And nothing else.

"Ah, Duncan, is that you? How nice of you to come," said Uncle Dudley's partial head. "Don't be alarmed. Well, I mean, don't be *unnecessarily* alarmed. You aren't, are you?"

"Wh—wh—wh—" I replied.

"Just ran into a bit of complication, you see," the mouth went on. "Hoping you might lend a hand."

And it grinned, pleasantly.

And this is how I learned the significance of the name Dr. Julius Feathergold, of the Knichtbubel Institute, and of his *Bulletins.* Dr. Feathergold was a rare scholar of arcane sciences and practices, you see, meaning an expert on mysterious things that very few people know about. You could call them alchemy or magic, plain and simple. Except they were hardly plain and simple! Dr. Feathergold would send reports (*Bulletins*) of his latest secret magical investigations to a special list of worthy readers/subscribers. One of these subscribers was my uncle Dudley.

These were the sort of researches my uncle was here in Mt. Geranium boning up on!

Dr. Feathergold's latest *Bulletin,* which I had so innocently carried upstairs the previous day, was all about his not-quite-finished inquiries into the "Science of Disappearance and Reappearance."

What Uncle Dudley had done was to rush into secret research conspicuously stamped:

WATCH IT!
NEEDS FURTHER TESTING!

He'd simply gone chanting away at "scientific incantations" (spells were what they were) of flabbergasting, but untested, power!

The result was the "incomplete reappearance" talking to me on the plaid blanket, alongside Señor Recuerdo's dark little stare.

It was something to see, believe me.

Now Uncle Dudley's partial head and shoulders wanted me to please just continue pronouncing incantations for him, until he achieved "proper reappearance."

"Just find the pages in green ink I imagine are at your feet," I was told cheerfully. "Can't miss 'em!"

This was true. But given my state of emotion, gathering the pages took a while.

And now the real problems started. Dr.

Feathergold's scientific spells were jumbled over various pages and in various partial, trial versions. Like I said, the great genius of the Knichtbubel Institute hadn't quite worked everything out yet.

However, out of respect for his subscribers, he had supplied a special formula they might use to try to "straighten out the details" themselves.

Carefully.

If all this sounds complicated to you, think what it was like for me, barely a year into algebra, up in that jam-packed room with Uncle Dudley's goateed half-head coaching me on! Me stammering aloud from the pages of Dr. Feathergold's *Bulletin:*

"*Invicius Ponticius Supalicius . . . Magililili—*" I stammered. "*Lililiculus?*"

"That's a lad; now go to page seven, per instructions," I was informed. "And read every other word of the last two lines!"

"*Fulimuli?*" I struggled. "*Sacamaca—visio? . . . Alta—malta—*"

"No no, page *seven!*" I was corrected.

"But it *is* page seven!"

"Hmmm. Well then, page eight. Try that," suggested partial Uncle Dudley.

An hour went by like this.

There was a yelp of hope when Uncle Dudley's shirt front appeared—only to disappear again. His eyes, which would have let him take over the reading from me, never materialized. I struggled on. Then a terrible thing happened.

Right in the middle of mangling another spell,

I heard a little popping sound. And all that remained visible of my uncle was one nostril, and his lips and goatee.

"Ah, that's definitely not it," declared the lips calmly. "All right, let's try—"

Frantic, I began shouting out parts of spells and incantations higgledy-piggledy. Sweat poured down me, the inky words began to blur before my eyes. Señor Recuerdo's fierce little face glared at me. Finally it was all too much.

With a yell I twisted around, and with "Now, now, nephew—" in my ears from the calm voice on the bed, I yanked open the door and ran out of the room. I went careening down the stairs, still clutching Dr. Feathergold's *Bulletin,* and burst out into the hallway on the second floor.

And came to a complete stop.

"Duncan!" blurted Mr. Feeley. My old Cub Scout leader came slowly pulling himself up the top of the stairs' bannister at the other end of the hall. "What is going on? I've been knocking on the front door for twenty minutes. Is

everything okay? I thought I heard someone scream when I went by earlier!"

(So I *had* screamed when I'd opened the guest-room door.)

"Where's your Uncle Dudley? Isn't he here?"

And Mr. Feeley stopped on the landing and stared at me, his chest heaving from the climb and being overweight.

I stared back at him, my own chest heaving. For different reasons. I looked wildly up the attic stairs; I backed into the stairwell.

"Dunc?" said Mr. Feeley, who was the only person who ever used that disgusting nickname. He started walking toward me, his head tilted.

I panicked.

"Verso — wugimugimerso — nunifunilerso!" I blurted frantically. I gaped down at the green-inked pages in my grip. *"Mingi—singi—vilio . . . Astroputri—livio!"*

I retreated slowly up the stairs as Mr. Feeley closed in.

"Silnu! Rumpilnu!"

"Dunc!" cried Mr. Feeley. "Dunc, what in *heck*

is going on!" He reached up for me with a fat hairy hand—and stopped.

Totally.

I gawked at him. He stood motionless, arm out, not budging. Not breathing. His eyes staring at nothing behind his glasses. The short hair of his crewcut shiny with sweat.

I had turned Mr. Feeley into a statue.

CHAPTER THREE
blibus blatus etc.

So that's what I had accomplished in one afternoon, an eleven-year-old kid left in the care of
my uncle.

I was now alone in our house with one spellbound whole adult, and the mouth and nostril of
another. Not to mention a shrunken head.

What would you have done? Me, I just sat
down on the attic stairs, quaking. For some time.

Then I got up and edged around motionless
Mr. Feeley and went downstairs into the kitchen. I
was so thirsty I could have drunk up all of
Gumberry Creek. The kitchen made me feel
better—as if the world was still the regular old

summer world. And what was going on upstairs was just a weird dream in an afternoon nap. I stood at the back window, gulping down most of a pitcher of iced tea, hearing the comforting clunk of ice cubes against my plastic tumbler.

Then I just stared outside, panting and rubbing the sweat off my cheeks.

I was in a very difficult situation. I could hardly call my parents. And the idea of being stuck in the guest room with only a piece of Uncle Dudley to guide me was about as pleasant as taking a math exam in a sack full of worms. If you know what I mean . . .

I felt a strong urge to just shove open the back door and run off into the warm Mt. Geranium afternoon, to find my partner, Arthur, for a late-day ramble out to check our inner tube, and do some exploring too.

"You look *strange*," Arthur would probably say, being Arthur. His gray eyes narrowing. "What's up?"

"Nothing," I'd gulp with a shrug, my young mind still reeling from the nightmarish and beyond-belief complications upstairs.

"*What?*" Arthur would demand.

"Nothing!" I'd insist.

There'd be an intense pause as Arthur stared. And then sneered.

"You're *faking*," he'd scoff. "It's *nothing!*"

"That's right," I'd mutter, with a strange little laugh that would drive Arthur crazy. "*Nothing at all . . .*"

If he only knew!

But how could I trust another kid, especially Arthur, with the gruesome and astounding trouble Uncle Dudley had gotten us into?

Yes, that's all I wanted, like any other normal kid—to run off into the sunshine with Arthur and leave the dreadful doings upstairs far behind. With their dark secret all to myself, and Arthur dying of curiosity and suspicion.

But even there in the kitchen I could hear my name being called, faintly, from the third floor.

And somehow I just took a deep breath, a shaky one, and went slowly way back upstairs to face my difficulties. Bizarre and unfair though they were.

"Ah, there you are, young Duncan," said my

uncle's goateed lips, when I pushed open the door again. "Refreshed, I hope, and not given in to despair!"

I broke the news about Mr. Feeley—still there like a statue at the foot of the attic steps.

"That all? Not to worry," I was assured. Uncle Dudley was a big one for assurances.

And so we started all over again.

I wish I could say that I snuck down to my room for ten minutes and figured out by spectacular brain power and previously unrecognized talent the clue to the knotted-up puzzle Dr. Feathergold had left so tangled. But that's not what happened.

Instead, I just kept at it, first one version of a spell, and then another, and then another, and then another—until I was sick of the stupid sound of my voice, and frustration made me want to throw the pages out the window!

"Uncle Dudley, it's just not gonna *work!*" I squawked, hearing one more cheerful encouragement from the lips on the bed, one more "Let's take time to do things right, lad!"

I twisted away, clutching my throbbing head. I

punched my thigh. "I mean, *Blibus blatus,* I dunno, *lobimobiglobidus!*—it's all junk, it's too much, I can't do it!" Complete despair.

Of course when I turned back to the bed, I let out a scream. A monster grinned at me.

Uncle Dudley—back at full size.

"Ah, Duncan lad. *Good work there at the end,*" he said.

I slumped against the wall and slid slowly down to the floor, while Uncle Dudley knelt beside me and peered, perplexed.

After I'd recovered enough, I naturally wanted to figure out the problem of Mr. Feeley. He was still there as I'd left him. But Uncle Dudley announced he was famished after so many long hours of complicated research—that I must be too. And that we would address the matter of Mr. Feeley in proper time.

"First things first," he said. Which usually meant food or drink in my uncle's case.

So Mr. Feeley stayed spellbound on the second

floor while Uncle Dudley and I wolfed down a turkey TV dinner each, and then a serving of Salisbury steak (Uncle Dudley finished off half of mine because I was full). Only then, after a leisurely pipe, did my uncle stretch his long arms in front of him and crack his knuckles. Then we went on up and took hold of Mr. Feeley.

He was as stiff as if he were carved out of a log. We hauled him down the stairs like a piece of furniture—"Mind his head!" cried Uncle Dudley—and out into the backyard, and leaned him up against the garage. Uncle Dudley put a glass of his special rum-and-milk punch in Mr. Feeley's hand (punch being every seafarer's favorite drink). Which I replaced with iced tea, remembering that Mr. Feeley didn't drink alcohol.

"Now what?" I said, as we stood there in the early evening, considering things.

"Now a little word of Dr. Feathergold's sagacious hocus-pocus, and we're home free," my uncle replied. Very casually, he began to chant.

"You know how to do this?" I blurted.

"*This* is child's play," he informed me with a wink.

Suddenly Mr. Feeley swayed, and splashed his iced tea. "Where—where am I?" he mumbled.

"Feeley!" cried Uncle Dudley. "Are you all right, old sword? You look a little rusty. Why you're here in the Peckle backyard, of course! Having looked in on young Duncan and myself, most graciously."

Mr. Feeley stood swaying, dumbly blinking at Uncle Dudley and then me. "Say . . ." he started to declare, slurring.

"Duncan, let's help our guest to a chair. What's in that iced tea?" my uncle joked.

Mr. Feeley gazed teetering down at his tea, while Uncle Dudley put his arm around his waist and began steering him slowly in the direction of the maple tree, where I was putting out lawn chairs.

And after we were all seated safe and sound, I watched as Uncle Dudley—all of Uncle Dudley—patted Mr. Feeley on the knee, and clinked glasses with him, and showed him the authentic whalebone of his pipe. And then treated us to the full moonlit saga of certain sea adventures along the old Panama Canal, down there

Valparaíso way. Which, of course, I already knew all about.

If Arthur had been lucky enough to be there, he'd probably have piped up about geographical technicalities. Being Arthur.

I just shook my head and sighed. I mean, how could anybody care about silly technicalities when it came to Uncle Dudley?

CHAPTER FOUR
music and cookies

So Dr. Feathergold's dangerous new *Bulletin* was stuffed away somewhere in the third-floor guest room—carefully, of course, "with only the greatest respect." To wait for "further boning up on . . ."

And my long Mt. Geranium summer days continued, under the care of my *in loco parentis.*

My parents called from Ohio to tell me how much they missed me and wanting to know how I was, and then wanting to know how I *really* was. Because my father had talked to Mr. Feeley, and

Mr. Feeley had sounded kind of strange. Uncle Dudley took over and assured them everything was "as smooth as the silk of the Emperor of Siam!"—that I was *flourishing* (he gave me a long wink), that Mr. Feeley had paid us the most *cordial* of visits (another wink), and we looked forward to more.

Then his face dropped, and I knew what was up as I took the heavy black receiver from him.

"Oh, hi, Aunt Mac," I said dimly. "I said, hi. Aunt Mac, it's me, Duncan—*Duncan*," I shouted. *"It's Duncan! Hi!"*

You always had to go through this with Aunt Mac, who was deaf but refused to fix her hearing aid. Of course she wanted to know all about my cello lessons.

My parents came back on and told me they'd write lots of postcards from their road trip, which they were about to start. My mother said that people in Cincinnati supposedly ate chili with chocolate sauce, could I imagine, and promised to bring home a jar. ("Yuck" was my reaction.)

After I'd hung up, Uncle Dudley slapped me on the shoulder.

"Come on, young glum fella! Let's go cheer ourselves up with a stroll along the boulevards of Mt. Geranium town!"

But I had to decline this new favorite activity.

"Gotta practice," I muttered, head sunk. "Got a cello lesson today." And I started clumping upstairs, with Uncle Dudley sighing in sympathy behind me.

"Courage!" he called out, as he went on to the third floor, to change from his stained robe into his patched-up tweed jacket. *"Remember heroic Horatio at his Roman bridge!"*

Now, I wouldn't exactly call my cello a horde of bloodthirsty barbarians, which was what this Horatio hero of Uncle Dudley's faced in ancient days. More, I'd say, a kind of endless, dreary pain. A cruel weight on my young spirit.

I just wasn't meant for the cello, you see. And the cello knew this, and my parents did too, I'll bet, but they felt obligated to go along with Aunt Mac's ambitions for me: my cello and lessons were her Christmas gift.

Some gift.

So for a half-hour that summer day I practiced

scales, and winced. Then I started slicing away at "Twinkle, Twinkle, Little Star" (after six months this was the glorious level of my cello-ing). But pretty quickly I gave up and snuck over to my desk to finish inking the new Gumberry Salvage Corp. official T-shirt. My logo redesign had been formally approved by my partner, Arthur, after some touchy debate. It now included the image of a shrunken head.

Arthur did not have a cello in his life. He had a clarinet. But he liked his clarinet, and his clarinet was flattered and liked him back. At that very minute he was probably honking away happily in his room.

Gloomily I buttoned up my cruel weight (my cello) in its carrying cover. As I came clumping through the front hall with it, I heard noises from the kitchen.

Strange, curious noises . . .

"Uncle Dudley?"

It was he, back from his stroll already and wearing, of all things, one of my mother's aprons! The curious noises came from the bowl and saucepans he was clattering around. I stared from the doorway with my cello as he whipped away at something with a big metal spoon, splattering himself with flour. Exotic packets sat open everywhere on the counter. I'd seen them before—up in the third-floor guest room.

"Duncan lad, the moon goes full tonight!" he announced, snatching up a wooden roller, which he rubbed wildly with more flour. "And I just now recalled a scrap of gypsy lore I'd heard tell of, from a strange fella I met once, on a car-avan by the Caspian Sea. Yes, you go make beautiful music, nephew of mine," he declared, "and afterward, we'll lure us some little full-moon visitors—with what I'm cooking up now, with a dash of these special Knichtbubel flavorings!"

It turned out the Knichtbubel Institute also offered subscribers a "select" line of powders, potions, and spices.

"Off you go, Horatio, off you go!" Uncle Dudley cried, and he spun around and flipped down the door of the oven with a flourish.

Well, guess what: my partner, Arthur, may have actually enjoyed going off to his music lessons. But for sure he wasn't sent on his way with the promise of such marvels in his ears!

How could he be? He lacked my marvelous uncle!

On this much happier note I clumped out into the lazy sunshine. At the corner, Mr. Feeley paused with his clippers and gave me a faint wave over his hedge, and then turned and stared off toward my house, frowning and rubbing his chin.

I went left on Myrtle Drive, along toward the campus of Mt. Geranium College and its music building.

I was reflecting how much the moon meant to Uncle Dudley. How, thanks to him, I'd become more properly moon-conscious myself, after so many ignorant years when I'd barely noticed it there among the stars—had taken practically for granted its gleaming queenly bubble (as Uncle Dudley called it) up in the night sky! As if it weren't the face really of a whole other world glowing down at my own gazing face. Arthur knew the names of mountains on the moon; his dad had given him a fancy telescope for his birthday. But mostly, before the telescope broke, he tried to look into people's windows.

And I wondered who those "little full-moon visitors" could be that Uncle Dudley talked about luring. Were they gnomes or elves?

Gnomes and elves . . . in Mt. Geranium?

These thoughts distracted me until I saw the college buildings up ahead. Then my stomach said, "Okay, enough," and went back to sinking.

It sank because of my music teacher, Linda Cooch. Linda Cooch was going to be a senior. She wasn't amazingly beautiful, not by regular standards, I imagine. But she had the most remarkably golden hair. It hung long and flat and shining over the collar of her blouse.

And she was almost as shy as I was. Which made us an excruciating total of shynesses.

By the end of our weekly hour together (once a month in summer, thankfully), I would often be so

twisted up because of her golden hair and her awkward manner that I'd manage to back onto, or step into, my cello.

And my father would have to drive me and Aunt Mac's evil generous gift back to the repair shop yet one more time.

"God in heaven, I cannot understand how an intelligent boy of eleven can keep trampling an instrument!" my father would mutter.

But on this particular summer afternoon, I somehow managed to escape any cello disaster. Perhaps it was my uncle's call for courage. Or the distraction of who might come calling under the full moon. Whatever it was, I scraped through my scales, and then through "Twinkle, Twinkle, Little Star," at which Linda Cooch winced slightly and said very softly, smiling, "A lot of that was almost in tune!" She giggled, and I gulped as she repositioned my hands, giggling some more — but no destruction! I packed my cello, and murmured goodbye, and then made it out the doorway and down the music building steps, cello under arm —

Safely.

I trudged back through the afternoon sunshine, grinning in triumph. Some aspiring young musicians might take pride in the awesomeness of their playing. Me, I was all puffed up because I hadn't destroyed my instrument!

So I was in a fine mood, maybe a little worn out, when I reached our front hall again.

And was greeted by an extraordinary smell coming from the kitchen.

"Uncle Dudley?"

But the kitchen was empty, except for the heap of pots and pans, washed and piled up from my uncle's cooking efforts.

And the plate of golden cookies, sitting there right in the middle of the kitchen floor.

From this plate an aroma entered my nose and thrilled every piece of me.

It was the most delicious smell I had ever experienced. Anywhere. Ever!

Hardly hesitating, I leaned down with my cello and picked up a cookie. The taste was every bit as sensational as my nose promised: warm nuggets of caramel, toasty cashew bits. I finished the cookie—what a dumb term, *cookie,* for something so marvelous!—and I took another—and then, as if under a spell, another. And before I knew it, every bit of baking magic on the plate was gone.

I was just chewing blissfully through the final mouthful, when I realized I wasn't alone.

A little husky man, hardly more than a foot tall, stood in the door of the pantry, scowling at me, his nose twitching.

A very odd little man in a dirty miniature suit of burlap, buttoned up tight, with a colored scarf around his throat and a hat like a puffy acorn on his bushy ginger head. He looked like he'd spent the night sleeping under a hedge (which, in fact, he had). The dusty skin of his round cheeks was covered in freckles. He had a bushy beard under his chin.

But his ears were the most eye-catching. They were much too big for his little round head. One ear had a big pointy tip, the other appeared partly bitten off.

I noticed all this during the long second's pause before the little man demanded fiercely:

"Watcha eatin'?"

I gulped, swallowing down what he was asking

about. "I . . . I . . ." I began faintly, but the little man interrupted with a shriek.

"Those are my cookies—*mine, mine!*" he squealed.

And he ran across the kitchen tiles in his dirty boots, and threw himself at my ankle, punching and chomping with his teeth.

I yelled and stumbled backward. "Quit it!" I shouted, shaking my leg and hopping, and swinging down wildly with my free hand. My attacker's teeth were too blunt and his fists too small to do any damage; but it was still a big shock.

And I still had the cello with me; after my day of triumph, I was determined it wouldn't suffer. I clung to it with all my might and tried to shake the little man off, and gradually I lost my balance as I hopped and in slow motion sank down, twisting, onto the kitchen floor, with Aunt Mac's gift cradled in my arms.

The little man started to climb up along me. "Help!" I yelled. "Help!"

Suddenly a voice roared and a broom swept across everything. The puffy acorn hat went flying. So did my attacker.

By the time I managed to get back up, Uncle Dudley had the little man pinned beside the empty plate on the floor. I put my cello away in a corner, then found some string from my mother's utility drawer, as Uncle Dudley instructed.

"Why in blazes a *goblin* here?" he muttered, as he tied up the squirming prisoner's little wrists. He sat back on his floppy heels, stroking his goatee.

"I'm really sorry, Uncle," I said sheepishly, nodding at the empty saucer. "They were just so deli—"

But he shut me off with a cry. "Unless I mixed in *caramel* and *cashews*, instead of *carob* and *cranberries!*"

"Oh, I *love* cashews—no! I *adore* them!" the little man gurgled.

"They're *the best*," I murmured myself, but discreetly.

"By the seven veils of Damascus!" said Uncle Dudley, and he squeezed his fist in annoyance. "I've misfabricated the enticement! 'Carob and Cranberry to lure an Elf/Caramel and Cashews for a Goblin's Call.' Oh, what a fool I am!" He looked at the floor and slapped his forehead. Another Knichtbubel "complication."

An alarming fear suddenly crept over me. "Uncle?" I asked, in a spooked voice. "Are there (gulp) any bad side effects from eating all the cookies 'for a Goblin's Call'?"

A question I'll bet my parents wouldn't have been too happy to hear me ask my *in loco parentis.*

"What?" Uncle Dudley muttered, distracted. "Oh, no no—feel a little odd, perhaps, that's all. But afraid your appetite has just put this fella in a nasty mood," he declared. "And a goblin's temper is bad enough as it is. Not sweet and cordial like an elf's."

As if on cue, the goblin banged his boot heels on the floor.

But there was nothing to be done. Every last cookie was gone, and it was too late now for any more magical baking, which has to be performed at the height of the day of a full moon.

Uncle Dudley sighed glumly. He'd have to wait a whole month if he wanted to try again at summoning a more cordial elf, which is what he had in mind. He'd never done it before.

I myself felt glum for the misery I'd caused the goblin by my greediness.

I knelt a safe distance from the pintsize fellow and looked at him. His little mouth was bunched in a scowl; a tear trickled over his dirty freckles.

"Oh, he's crying!" I whispered to Uncle Dudley.

My uncle crouched beside me and handed the goblin his acorn hat. The goblin squinted at us and sniffed loudly, and began his sad tale.

~ THE GOBLIN'S SAD TALE ~

"My name is Abraham Basket (said the goblin). Honest Abe Basket. You can ask anyone in the little kingdom, that's what they'll tell you. Go ahead and ask em! ("All right, we might," replied Uncle Dudley.) All right, then! (said Abe Basket). I may be ill-tempered, at times, but everyone will vouch I'm honest!

"My life has never been an easy one, no, never. And that's why the loss of a whole plate of yummy cookies is such a terrible awful blow to bear! ("I'm really *really* sorry," I murmured.) Because I'm an orphan, you know. My parents were killed in the great blue wheelbarrow disaster, whose deluge of bricks killed many! Red bricks, they were. Bright red chimney bricks! I was thrust into the harsh world at a tender age, with no one to love me—cast out on the stony brown ground and the sallow yellow meadows, with only the company of my shivery silvery tears—a child's shivery silvery tea—"

With a shout Uncle Dudley slapped him in the head. He grabbed Abe Basket's hair, and twisted his little neck this way and that.

"Desist!" he cried, as I gaped. "He's casting a spell with colors! Desist right now!" he snarled.

Honest Abe squirmed and twisted and sputtered on with "shivery silvery tears—shivery silvery tears—" until my uncle took hold of his good, pointy ear.

By then the kitchen around us was all chaotic with windows slamming down and up, curtains flapping, water gushing from the faucet.

"Not my ear, not my ear!" howled the goblin.

"Then swear on it!" snarled Uncle Dudley. "Swear or I'll twist it off, and chop it up for the robins and the squirrels to dine on!"

The goblin swore on his ear, sputtering.

"Now swear 'on my good ear,' " demanded my angry uncle, giving a shake.

"I swear—on my good ear!—to halt my spell. Ow!"

"All right, that'll stop things where they are," Uncle Dudley panted. "But hurry, Duncan. There's turmoil about us!"

So after turning off the kitchen tap, I went racing off through the rest of the house, which was in a frenzy. Roaring water was already spilling over in my parents' bathroom and in the one Uncle Dudley and I shared. Windows slammed up and down until I bolted them. Every mirror had slid to the floor and all my mother's flowerpots were tipped over.

I tidied what I could quickly. The house had a spooky, creepy feeling, like someone else was lurking about. I hurried back down to the kitchen. Abe Basket sat glum and silent in the middle of the floor. His acorn hat lay squashed beside him.

"Well, we're secure enough," said Uncle Dudley. "Once he's sworn like that, he can't go back on his word."

"Uncle!" I yelled, pointing. Something in the doorway had suddenly caught my eye.

"Come out," demanded Uncle Dudley. "I've a big broom handy. Come out!"

After a moment, another little person stepped into view. The female version of the goblin on the floor, with a long patched skirt, and ginger hair done up in fat braids, and the same freckles on her dusty cheeks. And two fine oversize pointy ears.

She stared up at us, and suddenly her face crumpled into immense sorrow and she dropped the armful of my mother's thimbles and ribbons and sewing yarns she was carrying.

"My name is Hettie Buckle," she began, with a sob in her voice. "Honest Hettie Buckle. You can ask anyone in the little kingdom, that's what they'll tell you. Go ahead —"

"It's no use, Hettie," grumbled Abe Basket from the floor. "I've sworn on my ear."

"Just go ahead and ask 'em," Hettie Buckle continued pitifully, a tear trickling over her

freckles. "I'm an orphan, you know, my life has never been an easy one, never, that's why the loss of such shiny, pretty, lovely—"

"On my good ear, Hettie!" declared Abe Basket.

"Oh . . ." said Hettie Buckle, and she stopped, and sniffed, and looked really very sad.

And there we were, Uncle Dudley and me, with two miserable little people on our hands. Stuck with them till the morning dew, which every Feathergold subscriber knows is when, and only when, little guests can be asked to leave. Even bad-tempered little guests.

"Well, well." Uncle Dudley tugged at his goatee as he pondered what to do.

"We're honest, you know!" Abe Basket announced again.

"We are, indeed!" said Hettie Buckle, who sat on the kitchen floor with her arm around him. "And we'll make amends for any harm. We're goblins, and proud of it!"

And they together stuck out their dusty chins.

So Uncle Dudley decided to take them at their word. Abe Basket was untied, after being reminded he'd sworn on his ear. He and Hettie were put to work to clean up the mess he'd enchanted.

But goblins aren't much use at cleaning, because of their small size, and because they tend to be careless and distracted by smells and bright things. They're not really talented when it comes to chores.

By now evening was here. It had been a long eventful day, even for a summer of long eventful days.

We put the goblins out in the backyard, to spend the night in the open as they were used to doing. For supper we gave them graham-cracker pieces, with a splash of condensed milk, in paper cones. "Just a splash now," said Uncle Dudley. "The lactose in the milk makes 'em tipsy."

Then he put away the pots and pans while I hauled my cello up to the safety of my room. I fixed up a few more overturned flowerpots. But I hadn't much talent really for chores myself. Not with actual goblins around!

After dinner, I joined Uncle Dudley in "being sociable" to our guests out by the maple tree.

The moon had risen up through the stars, and now it shone its luminous glow down on Clover Crescent. We sat on the grass, the four of us, gazing up with the crickets all around and Uncle Dudley's pipe smoke drifting over our heads.

"Oh, it's such a pretty shiny thing!" whispered Hettie Buckle, wonder and longing in her voice.

Uncle Dudley in his Panama told us the story of three very brave men he knew personally, who'd set off for the moon in a special boat, and had gotten partway. "You can see the dent their oars made, at that very spot in the night sky," he declared. The rest of us gazed where he pointed with his pipe, but couldn't make it out.

Then Uncle Dudley and Abe Basket discussed what the moon was *really* made of, each offering their analysis. Very different from what Arthur would've said, I'm sure, poor know-it-all Arthur. I talked to Hettie Buckle, and out of politeness—and curiosity, because I'd never met goblins before—I asked her where she lived.

Well, she said, the big weedy ditch by Farmer Swenson's field was one of her favorite places—did I know it? I had to shake my head. "Or the Great Puddle by the graveyard—perhaps you know that?"

I didn't. But she hadn't heard of Gumberry Creek herself.

So I switched topics and asked her if she and Abraham Basket were married, and did they have any goblin children? To which she made a hoot and said, "Married, on my life!"—and then suddenly she looked very sad and she turned to her little man and took his hand and squeezed it and stroked it and sniffed. And I murmured another apology. I did a lot of apologizing that afternoon and evening.

Uncle Dudley poured out "a touch more" condensed milk, to be the good host, and things got lively. One of our guests, I can't recall which, asked for music.

"Well, now!" replied Uncle Dudley. "We happen to have a very brilliant young musician here in our midst!"

So I was persuaded to go inside for my cello. And this was how I came to scrape out "Twinkle, Twinkle, Little Star" for the third time in one day, sitting in a lawn chair in the moonlight.

There was a brief interruption of barking from the other side of the hedge.

"That's not a *terrier*, is it!" cried Abe Basket, rushing away to the garage and cowering there, clutching his bad ear.

"No, it's Slipper, the Beachams' spaniel," I assured him.

"As long as it's not a *terrier!*"

"Hello there. What's going on? Everything all right?" called Mr. Beacham's voice over the hedge.

"All fine. Just a little backyard soiree," Uncle Dudley called back.

After a pause, a confused "Oh . . . well, all right" came back, and we could hear Mr. Beacham escorting Slipper back into the house.

Our soiree resumed, a little quieter but still lively. The goblins got up to dance, tipsily. My version of "Row, Row, Row, Your Boat," which was the other tune I could play, had several encores. Then Abe Basket fell on his butt and Hettie Buckle laughed at him, and he kicked at her with his boots, so Uncle Dudley had to break it up. Then she fell over, and he laughed, and she kicked him, which called for breaking up again. Finally the two of them fell over together and just lay making senseless milky noises in the grass.

Uncle Dudley grinned down at the scene and announced that our soiree was finally at an end. And I packed up my cello one more time.

Up in bed, I lay deep in my pillow. But sleep wouldn't come. The face of my partner, Arthur, kept dreamily appearing, scowling in envy of my musical successes and all the astonishing events he knew not one iota about. (Not that I cared, of course.) I got up, pulled a chair by the window, and sat with my chin on my arms, yawning out at the moon through the curtains. I gazed at it with a tender intensity that was new to me, and I thought it resembled a golden goblin cookie. (That deliciousness still remained faintly in my mouth.) I sighed, or something like that. A lovely shiny thing, it was, the moon. . . .

Like Linda Cooch's golden hair . . .

The sudden image of my blond music teacher, there in my bedroom, made me grin with dizzy awkwardness. I gulped and shifted in my seat.

Then I thought of the pintsize visitors out in the backyard. Of the longing on Hettie Buckle's little face as she gazed at the moon.

I thought of it, and I got up. I went over to my bureau and selected the shiniest quarter in my wallet.

I crept down to the dark kitchen, where I washed the quarter stealthily in dish detergent. Then I rubbed it dry. Until it gleamed.

Under the maple tree, an apple crate sat tipped on its side as a bed for our visitors, who had borrowed a kitchen towel for a blanket. I crept close, hearing the snores from the heap of dusty burlap arms and legs and kitchen towel and ginger heads. Silently as I could, I reached out to lay the quarter in the grass where it would be found in the morning. Something that turned out to be a braid moved in the snoring heap. Hettie Buckle's little swollen eyes blinked at me.

Her eyes saw the bright quarter, and they widened. I gestured with the coin that it was for her. Her hands struggled out and seized hold of it. She gazed in wonder. "Oh, bless your heart, kind sir," she cried softly, and she pulled the quarter to her chest. "Bless your heart!"

I'd never been called "sir" before, and not by a woman, however small, who was also crying quiet tears of gratitude. I didn't know what to do. I started to say, "You're welcome," but it didn't seem right. I couldn't apologize again. So I just grunted, "That's okay," and shrugged, then crept back toward the house through the moonlight.

Uncle Dudley was waiting at the back door. He nodded and smiled. "Got a good heart, Duncan lad," he said, as we plodded through the kitchen to the stairs. "Yes, a good heart," he repeated, clomping along in untied shoes. The laces had been stolen just now, somehow.

But how much do shoelaces cost? Not much more than a quarter, really.

And so on up we went, to our beds.

And the backyard was sunny and empty at breakfast.

CHAPTER FIVE
above old Nanking

My parents were still away on their lazy road trip home.

Maybe *lazy* isn't the right word, since practically every day I received a postcard from them reminding me to say hi to Mr. Feeley and "trusting" that Uncle Dudley was "behaving responsibly." The postcards made a kind of photo model of their journey—3-by-5-inch waterfalls and soldier statues, panoramas of state parks and the ruins of early settlements attacked by Hachitee or Chicamunk or Laughing Fox Indians.

But, unfortunately, no horses or old post offices!

That combo was a great passion of mine, which I haven't yet mentioned. There was a brand-new show on TV called *"Hiyo" Harry of the Pony Express!* and every Tuesday night I'd be there in front of our set, to witness another tale of the fearless young man who delivered the mail "through the harrowing hazards of the Western Frontier!"

I could barely wait for Wednesday mornings— any other mornings and afternoons too—to leap on my bicycle and rush off *"Hiyo!"*-ing in the direction of Arthur's house. I was fearless Harry Whipple Jr. a hundred years in the future, furiously racing the 1.6 miles of Mt. Geranium streets past hostile parked cars and chasing dogs, to where Arthur would be waiting with a change of mounts (his bike), to send me back on the return leg. I carried an old Cub Scout backpack full of fake U.S. and territorial mail.

Then Arthur would come racing back and

forth on his turn, and we would compare times. Gumberry Salvage Corp.'s inner tube became sadly neglected.

"So how's your uncle?" asked Arthur, panting after yet another losing effort. "Still busy making those fancy paper hats for sitting out in the dark?" And he snorted, in his ignorance. Arthur thought he was being snide sometimes.

"He's been doing . . . lots of things," I sniffed. And I tried not to smile. "Hey," I said, changing the subject, "did you know that Johnny Utah, who sings the *'Hiyo' Harry* theme song, actually once lived here in Mt. Geranium?"

"Are you kidding?" sneered Arthur. "It was me who told you!"

Arthur was fine for topics like that, you see. But there was no way a regular kid like him could handle all the magical amazements that had come into my life thanks to Uncle Dudley. I could barely comprehend them myself.

Uncle Dudley was not a TV type, but he watched an episode of *"Hiyo" Harry* with me. "Undeniably heroic," he admitted, after our hero had dodged arrows and bullets to deliver medicine to a sick homesteader baby—and then galloped on with a love letter from a desperate young lady to her fiancé, an army lieutenant stranded without mail at a fort on the warpath.

"Unexpectedly touching . . ." he added, tapping at his eyes with the back of a hand. He could get emotional at times, Uncle Dudley.

Besides *"Hiyo"*-ing, my other favorite activity just then was to go strolling with my *in loco parentis*—to hear him spin yarn after yarn, and even sing, in a faint voice, when we followed the path that ran along Gumberry Creek by the girls' college hockey fields.

Our main strolling route, of course, was along the way into town center. People would turn their heads and slowly scratch them at the sight of Uncle Dudley. He had a habit of wearing his tweed jacket like a cloak around his bony shoulders. It was super-sophisticated for Mt. Geranium, along with his Panama hat. To be honest, if my dad had gone out looking like that, I would have found a hole to crawl in.

But alongside a "world voyager" like Uncle Dudley, I felt a kind of cocky pride, even if my eleven-year-old face did feel a little warm and red at the time.

Our first strolling stop in town was usually The Reader's Friend secondhand bookshop. Mr. Adamzicki, the proprietor, had hair in his ears and wore old colored suspenders over his shirtsleeves. He was a very quiet, thoughtful man, but somehow he and Uncle Dudley became friends right away. Like my uncle, he smoked a pipe, and together they would sit in the rear of the musty bookshelves, puffing away over a chessboard. Uncle Dudley would go on about "Queen's-

Pawn-Sacrifice Defense Number Three!" and "Bing-Schwarznut False-Knight Gambit Number Five!" and all sorts of other fancy chess talk. And quiet Mr. Adamzicki would checkmate him every time. But my uncle made Mr. Adamzicki smile. I think he sympathized with the special one-of-a-kind spirit of Uncle Dudley.

Because of this sympathizing, one afternoon Mr. Adamzicki brought out a book that had come in, which he'd picked out just for Uncle Dudley on account of my uncle's passion for bubbles.

Bubbles! . . .

Maybe I mentioned, Uncle Dudley was *obsessed* by them. He considered bubbles nature's and

man's "highest and finest expression." He regarded them the best design in the universe for anything at all you might want to do. His own book, the one that existed only in Japanese, was supposedly all about bubbles.

Now he gasped, and stared at the dusty volume in his hands. " *Bubble Riders of Old Nanking*!" he read aloud, his voice soft with delight. "By the seven lamps of Borneo, I'd heard of such when I was wintering one time by the China Sea!"

And then he made the fateful mistake of bringing up the Pony Express.

"See here, Duncan lad? Your Hopalong Harry

(my uncle was a real name-muddler), all swift and gallant, to be sure. But earthbound! Regard these postal messengers from lost Imperial days— zipping along the tides of air on nature's supreme vehicles!"

And a sparkle of inspiration came into his eye.

I peered at the open page.

And that sparkle in his eye unfortunately spread across to me.

To be fair to Uncle Dudley in all that happened afterward, I have to say he never really meant to involve me in his scheme, as he searched through the back of the book and found, to his extra delight, a bunch of technical suggestions. In fact, the opposite: at first he wouldn't hear of me taking any part.

But who wants to be *alone* enjoying marvels? Nobody, I bet.

Uncle Dudley immediately purchased *Bubble Riders of Old Nanking,* on credit, of course.

Without lingering for chess, we set off, both excited, for our customary second stop: the lunch counter at Kefauver's Five and Ten.

Kefauver's was a sleepy old-time variety store with a stale smell in the air and a sad bunch of things on its shelves. Hardly anybody went there anymore, except for some of the old folks who refused to shop anywhere else.

Uncle Dudley went (and me with him) because it was cheap. But mostly because of Dot Bunkmeier, the lunch-counter waitress.

Have I talked about her before? Uncle Dudley had met her soon after he arrived. To say he felt about Dot—or Dorothy, as he called her—the same way I felt about Linda Cooch would be unfair. Uncle Dudley didn't destroy anything on a regular basis. He wasn't tongue-tied.

But he did always gulp a lot before entering the store, and readjust his jacket around his shoulders, and fuss with the frayed neck of his collarless striped shirt "custom-made in Hong Kong." And touch the spot on his sleeve under which lay the heart tattooed on his arm.

"Aloha, dearest Dorothy!" he cried, as we took our seats at Kefauver's worn Formica counter.

"Well, hello there, fine gents!" Dot called back, and came over, smiling, with a couple of

menus for us. As a courtesy only; our order was always the same.

Dot Bunkmeier was not someone you might expect to stir up Uncle Dudley's emotions. She was a big, healthy woman with a sunny laugh, and a tan to go with it, which she got from her hobby, hiking.

She hiked with her husband, whose name was Stu. They had recently moved to Mt. Geranium.

Dot didn't know many other local people yet, so she welcomed Uncle Dudley's visits in a friendly way and didn't take his fancy compliments too seriously. Not having kids of her own, she took a shine to me.

"How's the real 'Hiyo' Harry today?" she asked, mussing my hair as I bent over the engravings in *Bubble Riders of Old Nanking*, which I'd had the privilege to carry from The Reader's Friend.

"Fine," I mumbled.

"'Fine'?" said Dot. "Gee, doesn't sound like you mean it!"

I grinned, only half-listening.

"*Bubbles*," declared Uncle Dudley. "*The magic of bubbles!*"

Magic, oh yes! Ponies and bicycles were terrific things—but here before me were:

Flocks of daring young men in pajamas and slippers and little black caps . . . riding the very air astride giant bubbles! Hauling their postal pouches high over the sprawling old capital and its province, along the wind, through weather fair and foul, delivering the rice-paper mails!

Love letters, business documents, family news, you name it!

"Only terminated the service because of ill will from the carrier-pigeon owners," murmured Uncle Dudley, tugging his goatee as he read on over my shoulder. "Technology fundamentally sound. Just driven out of the sky by coordinated aviary harassment!"

"Bubbles, huh?" said Dot, placing our sandwich usuals before us (fishy tuna for Uncle Dudley, squashy grilled cheese for me).

"Divinest things in God's creation," exclaimed

my uncle. Then, blinking a couple times, he added, "Besides a lovely women's smile!" and blinked some more.

"Oh, you say the *darnedest*—" said Dot with a grin. The rest of the sentence was swallowed up in her sudden whoop of laughter, as she flapped at my uncle, who grinned himself, and then slowly picked at his goatee, his eye lingering on the wedding ring on Dot's tanned hand, which was spread beside her plastic nameplate above her heart.

These last details I only guess at, from previous lunches, since I wasn't looking. I was lost, that lunch, in the skies above old Nanking, reliving the terrible midair ambushes of the gallant bubble riders by hordes of enraged carrier pigeons. Bursting bubbles! . . . head-over-heels pajamas! . . . rice-paper mail swirling down like confetti!

But I know for a fact that by the time we left Kefauver's, we'd been invited to Dot and Stu's to try out their new cookout grill next evening.

And I know that Arthur beat me, badly, when we raced Pony Express before dinner.

"That was the biggest . . . margin of victory . . . *ever!*" he boasted, delighted and kind of stunned, as we stood panting with our bikes in front of his porch steps.

"So?" I shrugged, blinking away sweat.

"So you're a sore loser!" he said. He scowled at my lack of sportsmanship. "And what was that weird word you yelled instead of *Hiyo?*"

"That was *Con-gee-ee!*" I informed him. "That's what they'd shout, in old Nanking."

"*China?*" Arthur being Mr. Geography again.

"Of course. The bubble riders. They'd beat 'Hiyo' Harry so bad, it'd make you sick."

"Oh yeah?" said Arthur, bewildered but riled

up on behalf of the Pony Express and his new record. *"Oh yeah?"*

I just sniffed, and shrugged again.

Thanks to Uncle Dudley, you see, I wasn't satisfied anymore with regular boyhood stuff. My head was full of bubbles.

I rode home brooding on the metal heaviness of my vehicle.

But what on earth could I do about it?

My answer came from the bathroom. The one I shared with Uncle Dudley.

I was clomping up the stairs to my room when I heard funny thumps, and then another cry for help from along the hall. I hurried toward it and opened the bathroom door, and there I was gaping up at a bizarre and yet thrilling sight.

"Ah, Duncan lad," said Uncle Dudley. His Panama hat was somehow still on his head, despite the fact that he was suspended upside down from the ceiling—his arms wrapped around a large, glassy, glistening globe.

A bubble!

"Grab hold of me, nephew of mine, and bring us down, if you kindly would," he requested. "Just mind the hatchery!" He was referring to the bathtub, which steamed below him, full of water and greenish-colored foam.

Using a chair from my room to reach from, I was able to get a grip on some of my uncle's shirt and drag him awkwardly down toward the floor. At the last struggling moment he let go of the bubble—which shot back up, thumping against the ceiling as he went sprawling beside the tub.

"Strengthening compound works dandy!" he announced, getting to his feet and rubbing his elbow. "Expanding powder too. Ah, the genius of good old Knichtbubel Inst.! It never fails!"

I stared up in disbelief and awe. The big thin-skinned thing wobbled in place overhead. "It's just like—old Nanking!" I whispered to myself.

"Nanking comes to Mt. Geranium!" my uncle declared, eyes sparkling. "Or it will, once I calibrate a few things more exactly." And I heard then those terms I'd become so familiar with: *tensile* strength, *internal-pressure ratio*, and of course, *buoyancy dynamics.*

I took it all in, thrilled. "Uncle!" I cried. "You mean we'll actually be able to go riding on these bubbles!"

"*'We'?*" he replied. He shook his head. "No no. 'Fraid not, Duncan lad! We're a team in all things, my fine young nephew. But this is much too dangerous for a youth, even as fearless as yourself!"

He was right for once. Give Uncle Dudley some credit for that, despite what was to follow.

But I was bubble-mad and eleven years old. "Ah, come on, Uncle!" I protested. "I'll be careful. I'll wear protection—a helmet. And pads—and whatever!" I knew the importance of a show of specifics in such arguments.

Uncle Dudley smiled in sympathy but still shook his head. But I wouldn't give up.

"We can make a surprise," I made up desperately. "We can—meet Mom and Dad!—on the way here! They'll love it! We can surprise them!"

It was a ludicrous idea, one that any other *in*

loco parentis would have sneered at. But not Uncle Dudley.

"No no no—" he repeated at first. But when I explained excitedly that my mother and father would be staying the final night of their trip at their sentimental favorite motel, just a hundred miles away, a look came over him. A real Dudley look. "A surprise . . ." he murmured.

My uncle Dudley loved surprises.

He pulled at his goatee. "Well, perhaps . . . *Perhaps.* But only if I'm convinced it's absolutely safe, and aerodynamically sound! Really, I'll have to think about it."

"*Con-gee-ee!*" I whooped, in delight at his first signs of yielding.

"*Con-gee-ee!*" he repeated, grinning wide as I jumped up and down.

The two of us whooping away in the bathroom, with bubbles on the brain.

Then we set about deflating the bouncy globe overhead, which displayed far too much *buoyancy dynamics.* And, as it turned out, overdeveloped *tensile strength.* We had to ram at it with a crowbar

from the garage. At last it popped, with an ear-splitting soapy bang.

Uncle Dudley was still officially "thinking over" my midair permission when Stu Bunkmeier pulled up in his camper truck next evening, to take us to the cookout.

"Hey, those look great!" he said, nodding at the bouquet of droopy flowers in crinkly wrapping that was meant for his wife. Uncle Dudley held it up carefully, squeezed in the middle of the three of us in front, as we bounced along.

Stu was a solid cheery man with a limp. He was maybe not quite as sunny about everyone as Dot was. And he seemed a little bewildered by us, his cookout guests. Probably he was accustomed to the sort of people he worked with at Forrestal's Lumber Yard. But he tried to be sociable.

"Dot loves flowers, you bet," he declared. "Loves to pick 'em when we go hiking up Mt. G." Mt. G. being the actual, very small mountain nearby that our town was named for. "But she'll have to wait awhile now, since I sprained my knee Sunday." He grinned and shook his head.

Behind the bouquet, Uncle Dudley's eyes shifted about. A thought seemed to work in them.

"How calamitous," he said sympathetically.

Stu's head jerked back. "'Calamitous,'" he said. After a pause, he laughed strangely and looked at Uncle Dudley. "*Calamitous.* Well, I'll be—" He scratched the side of his jaw.

We waited to turn left into the new development of small pale-brick houses and cement driveways where the Bunkmeiers lived.

So, wondered Stu, clearing his throat loudly as we made the turn. Uncle Dudley ever do much hiking himself?

My uncle of course answered in his personal style, bringing up "the vistas of the Hindu Kush, the byways of the lesser Fjords." Also "treks across the Siamese Ridges." Not to mention "atmospheric rambles by Gumberry shores."

"Gee," said Stu, pulling in past a mailbox on a post. *"We have been all kinds of places—ain't we?"* And he cleared his throat hard, and grinned, very hard.

It was not a great start for a fun evening.

I didn't help it by asking for rice, after we'd been shown the "Bunk-house" backyard barbecue by Dot, who was dressed up in a pink terry-cloth jump suit that showed off her not-so-skinny figure. Which seemed to distract very much my uncle with his bouquet.

"*Oh, baked potato don't suit ya?*" said Stu, grinning some more. Foil-wrapped spuds sat heaped up by the juicy burgers and franks on the grill.

But rice was what bubble riders ate, I explained to Dot, while Uncle Dudley explained to Stu what exactly milk-and-rum punch was.

"So it's all bubbles now, and no more 'Hiyo' Harry?" said Dot, coming back out considerately stirring a saucepan of gooey instant rice.

This got me going in detail about the glories of the sky riders of old Nanking. And yet how amazing it was (I looked over toward Uncle Dudley), the safety and freedom from accidents of the "basic technology"!

"Gosh, sounds like you're planning on riding a bubble yourself!" said Dot.

"*No no!*" two voices, mine and Uncle Dudley's,

hastily disagreed. Even as an eleven-year-old, after all, I knew bubble riding wasn't for blabbing about in public. In fact most doings involving Uncle Dudley weren't.

But I'd made the mistake of mentioning the bubble riders' favorite cry.

"Congee," said Stu Bunkmeier suddenly. *"Con-gee-gee."* He grinned and blinked. He had a tall can of beer in his hand. "Hey, I like that: *"Con-gee-gee!"*

My uncle and I exchanged looks of dismay and distress. Hearing the call of the Nanking skies in someone else's mouth, especially mangled by Stu, was close to sacrilegious.

"Hey, Dud, how about a game of horseshoes?" cried Stu, slapping my uncle on the back so his rum punch splashed. *"Con-gee-gee!"*

"Now, Bun-bun," warned Dot, "you need to ask Mr. Dudley here if he minds being addressed like that. Some people would. But try it," she said to Uncle Dudley. "It's a great game, we love it!"

"Come on, Dudley, Dud, whatever," said Stu. "Let's see ya play! *Con-gee-gee!"*

I don't know if my uncle had ever played

horseshoes before. I'm certain he wanted to impress Dot. The trouble was that Stu Bunkmeier quickly discovered the effect of yelling, *"Con-gee-gee!"* when Uncle Dudley was taking his turn. Uncle Dudley would be in mid-toss, full of style, when Stu would yell, *"Con-gee-gee!"* and the horseshoe would shoot straight up, high in the 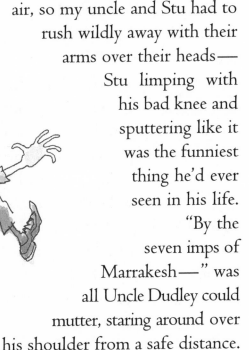 air, so my uncle and Stu had to rush wildly away with their arms over their heads— Stu limping with his bad knee and sputtering like it was the funniest thing he'd ever seen in his life. "By the seven imps of Marrakesh—" was all Uncle Dudley could mutter, staring around over his shoulder from a safe distance.

It was an awful thing to see.

When a horseshoe from my relative flew dangerously straight back over the chainlink fence, into the neighbor's marigolds, Dot finally called for Stu to stop. Though she was biting the grin on her lip.

Dinner went much the same way. *"Con-gee-gee!"* Stu kept squawking, rhythmically, like a haunted chicken. And Dot kept flapping at him and cheerily shushing. Harassed and distracted like this, my uncle and I both fell like circus clowns off the picnic bench we shared. First he got up without warning me, dumping me hard on the ground. Then I forgot and did the same to him.

We were splattered with drink and barbecue (and myself, rice) by the time Dot drove us home.

A real social failure, the cookout, you might think. Dot seemed to feel that way, as she apologized for Stu, who by the end of the evening had become a kind of weird zombie. He just sat there growling, *"Con-gee-gee . . ."* very quietly and nastily over his empty beer cans.

But Uncle Dudley felt otherwise. For one

thing he was now squeezed in the front seat against Dot, whom he could call "Dorothy" again without hearing somebody's beery cackle. He laughed away Stu's "shenanigans." And then steered talk to Dot's love of hiking—of picking flowers on Mt. G., which was visible in its glory from her kitchen window. These were topics he hadn't been able to bring up properly during the cookout.

Dot sighed. Yessir, she'd been looking forward to climbing to pick a certain blossom that grew on the top of Mt. G.: the famous "Mt. Geranium geranium" (not a proper geranium, actually; a type of edelweiss).

But now with Stu's knee so sprained . . .

We arrived at Clover Crescent. Dot squeezed a hand past my uncle to ruffle my hair, and thanked Uncle Dudley again for the bouquet, and Uncle Dudley took Dot's hand and kissed it, which made her bray like a donkey with laughter. And you would think here was the perfect opportunity for my uncle to suggest a hike up Mt. G.

But, like me, he was shy.

And being shy, he had a much grander flower scheme than just a hike clicking away in his brain.

A flower scheme that to my delight—and danger—involved me too.

CHAPTER SIX
D for derring-do

A flower scheme for love, or Uncle Dudley's version of it. And love turns out to be a feeling that can make an *in loco parentis* do truly idiotic, crazy, irresponsible things. Like permit a pleading eleven-year-old kid like me to go riding along in the skies.

But at least Uncle Dudley wasn't going to launch the two of us a hundred miles without some practice. Which is where his flower scheme came in.

"Before I even *contemplate* a long-distance surprise voyage to your parents," he declared the next morning, "we must first test our abilities on a practice flight."

A practice flight where? Why, up to the top of Mt. G.—to pick the geranium that grew there, which Dot Bunkmeier loved, and bring it back down here to our house on Clover Crescent! Our practice flight was a love errand, to fetch a gift to go between the pages of a book of poems my uncle would buy secondhand and on credit. And give as a gift to Dot at Kefauver's lunch counter.

That was his big flower scheme.

But all I cared about was that magic word of Uncle Dudley's: *we.* I leaped in the air like a bubble myself. Like the Nanking bubble hand-designed on my T-shirt, to replace the old logo of Gumberry Salvage Corp.

"*Con-gee-ee!*" I yelled, on a note of defiance after the Bunkmeiers' cookout.

"*Yes, con-gee-ee . . .*" my uncle answered, stroking his goatee, the glow of love scheming in his eye.

So we set to work—the two of us!—on "aero-vehicular research." There was a lot to be done. Up on the third floor, Uncle Dudley adjusted the blend of special soap powders from the Knichtbubel Institute's home supplies, to develop *bubble expansion* and *bubble strengthening,* according to the guide in the back of *Bubble Riders of Old Nanking.* I waited below in our bathroom laboratory by the filled tub, ready to *bubble hatch.*

"All right then, tireless nephew, now *this* ratio!" my uncle would declare, wiping at his stained fore- head with a stained hand as he sprinkled out yet another powder formula.

And I would stir furiously, and he'd scoop, and blow very carefully through the bubble maker (which looked like the frame of a kitchen sieve minus its meshing)—and then very skillfully he'd swing the bubble maker about, while I ducked out of the way, until the growing bubble swelled into a kind of glistening see-through beach ball. And then he'd snap it off with a flick of his wrist, like a lion tamer at a circus cracking a delicate whip. And I would lunge and trap this latest trial bubble in my arms, for inspection.

This is how at last we made a bubble with the proper *buoyancy dynamics* (it would hover but not rocket upward) and sufficient *tensile strength* (to bear weight—as well as squeezing, handholds, and jabs from small sharp objects).

I don't mean to boast, but it was a pretty impressive piece of research for a kid like me to be part of.

And now I could start practice-riding. What a thrill, to sit like a jockey on a Knichtbubelized bubble—in midair! Even if I was just hovering over my own staircase bannister above the front hall, and clunking my head against the ceiling after Uncle Dudley brought out the electric fan and turned it to high, four feet away, to imitate a wind current.

A thrill even when my uncle made me change

out of my pajamas and slippers and too-small Cub Scout cap. "But it's what they wore in Nanking!" I protested. Didn't matter. I had to bundle up in homemade safety gear: a bicycle helmet, pillows strapped front and back over layers of sweaters and jeans, and bunched-up socks for kneepads. Plus a safety rope (some of my mother's laundry line), to connect me to Uncle Dudley during actual flight high above Mt. Geranium.

I was now fat as a blimp, pouring sweat, and supposedly safe. And now, instead of hovering, I just sank, very very slowly on my bubble, twirling and bumping past the bannisters, onto the front-hall carpet.

"By the seven feathers of Omar's partridge . . ." muttered Uncle Dudley, watching from the top stair. He sat down and rubbed at his shirtsleeve over his tattoo, and brooded. "We've got a launching problem," he declared.

Bubble riding, you see, requires good strong air currents. And good strong air currents only move up high. Unless you happen to be near the ocean, where the wind always blows. In Nanking the riders launched from the lighthouse in the harbor. Or from a special tower built for them high in the hills beyond the city. High is the key.

◆　◆　◆

We on our Feathergold-formula Mt. Geranium bubbles couldn't *loft* from our backyard on Clover Crescent. Unless there was a gale, which was hardly riding weather. My uncle and I went up to check out the roof. But the breeze was no better there. And all around were power lines, TV aerials, chimneys.

Not to mention neighbors.

"A bit public, eh, for a grown man and an eleven-year-old boy to become spectacularly airborne," Uncle Dudley murmured to me, with a sly wink in the direction of Mr. Feeley's house. Bubblehead-in-training that I was, I winked slyly back.

So my uncle spent hours analyzing topographical maps of our area. And that is why, shortly before sunset two days later, Mr. Adamzicki from the bookstore pulled into the back of our driveway. And Uncle Dudley and I secretively wrestled our two gleaming soapy bubbles out the kitchen door and into the rear of Mr. Adamzicki's beat-up station wagon, among the heaps of books and old copies of *Okay!* magazine. And then off we drove, very carefully, toward the lower slope of Mt. G.

Where the breezes would be blowing!

Uncle Dudley had confidentially explained our plan for the evening's ride to quiet Mr. Adamzicki, his friend. Mr. Adamzicki had given the book that gave Uncle Dudley his inspiration, after all. But I don't think my uncle had dared tell Mr. Adamzicki yet about our more breathtaking and much riskier plan for a surprise voyage to my parents in their favorite motel. For which all this was supposedly "practice."

Uncle Dudley now sat upright in the front seat of the station wagon, full of daring and the heroic, adventurous spirit of the evening ahead. He also looked kind of weirdly swollen. Like a turtle.

Guest-room pillows bulged under his tweed jacket, and his narrow noble head was hidden under a wool stocking cap from Mr. Adamzicki. My uncle wore the cap pulled very low, with a handkerchief curiously tied around it. A big *D*—for *Dot*—was colored boldly on the handkerchief. Like the way *Chocklee's Encyclopedia* said knights of old wore their damsels' names on their shields.

I sat swollen myself in the back seat. I kept shoving my bicycle helmet up as it kept slipping annoyingly down over my eyes. I had a broom from the kitchen across my lap, to use as an extra precaution to ward off any birds that might be inspired by Nanking carrier pigeons.

Our Knichtbubel bubbles sat in the rear, wobbling and glistening and eager for flight.

Uncle Dudley twisted around to me, grinning as I fussed with my helmet. "Now fret you not, brave young Duncan!" he declared, waggling the pair of my mother's gardening shears with which he was going to snip a geranium, when we passed across the top of Mt. G. for a moment midflight. "By the seven horns of Valhalla, this thing'll be a snap! Good old Dr. Feathergold, eh? *Con-gee-ee!*"

I replied the same. And he winked.

It was a brave wink. A real Uncle Dudley wink.

A pretty foolish wink, really, since Mr. Adamzicki, as I mentioned, drove very carefully and slowly. He had a terrible sense of direction too, almost as bad as Uncle Dudley's. Between the two of them, we got lost, and only found the right road up the mountain after I managed to make myself heard about my knowledge from exploring Gumberry Creek with Arthur.

We pulled over at last, sputtering, onto a clear space along a curve. We were almost an hour behind schedule. It was nearly dark. Mt. G.'s shadowy upper slopes loomed above us. Below us lay the tiny roofs of Mt. Geranium in its little valley.

"See what I mean?" cried Uncle Dudley triumphantly as we all got out. "Breeze fresh as you'd want up here!"

It sure was. The breeze made the ends of his handkerchief stand up like rabbit ears. Our plan was to ride this breeze on our bubbles, like an escalator, up to the top of Mt. G., do our flower snipping, then turn around and glide back down to town and Clover Crescent. All unnoticed in the darkness.

But first, before anything else, we had to rope ourselves together.

Where was the rope?

I crawled around in the back seat, looking for it, hampered by my helmet. And darkness. Eventually I found the rope. By now it was much too dark to see properly, so Uncle Dudley and I waited in front of the station wagon while Mr. Adamzicki found the knob to turn on his headlights, which then blinded us. By the time we had the rope tied right, it was really very *very* dark.

Uncle Dudley gave Mr. Adamzicki our safety

flashlight, and we went around to the back of the station wagon and opened the door in the flashlight beam. We managed to block our bubbles from escaping, and then I knelt in and took hold of one. And banged my head against the door as I did. I lurched sideways, and the breeze suddenly gusted, and with Uncle Dudley shouting and grabbing at us, and Mr. Adamzicki just grabbing, my bubble and I went heaving off into the air.

And then jerked to a stop ten feet above, like an airborne dog on a leash.

"Steady as she goes!" cried Uncle Dudley, bracing himself in the gusts and hauling me slowly down by the laundry safety rope. Mr. Adamzicki reached out to catch me by my flapping shoe, which kicked him right in the nose, which sent his glasses and the flashlight flying.

So we had to wait while he crawled around to locate them, with Uncle Dudley shouting directions.

Finally I was brought down and "secured," meaning stuffed partway into the back of the station wagon. Where my broom had got to in all this I can't tell you.

Then Uncle Dudley leaned in and wriggled his bubble out. Now even Mr. Adamzicki shouted warnings as the breeze gusted again. Uncle Dudley tried to hop onto the bubble but instead went careening slowly sideways off balance—and suddenly yanked me out after him by our rope.

And yelling and flapping and frantically hanging on to our bubbles, the two of us shot away, out into the air over the treetops. With Mr. Adamzicki yelling at us from below.

Our plan, like I said, was to ride the breeze up to the top of Mt. G. It was a brilliant plan, we thought, masterfully devised by Uncle Dudley.

But the frisky breeze didn't think so.

And *frisky* is the wrong word: it was more *insane*, this breeze. It roared and swept us immediately away from the slopes of Mt. G., off into the night.

I don't know if my uncle ever yelled *"Con-gee-ee!"* I only managed part of it, I was too busy struggling. I never really got seated properly on my bubble, as the breeze whooshed us out over the

valley toward Mt. Geranium town. For the few moments that my helmet wasn't over my eyes, I saw the figure of Uncle Dudley ahead of me, somehow upright on his bubble, clutching on. His handkerchief rabbit ears spun on his head like propellers. He grinned back around at me, calm as can be despite the shock and alarm in his eyes. He kept jabbing a bony hand with the gardening shears off in one direction, as if that was where we should be steering: to snip geraniums! He kept shouting while wrestling his bubble to head the right way. All I ever heard was "By the sev—"

Then the breeze decided to quit fooling around, and it blasted a fed-up *whoosh* that rammed me full on sideways, so I capsized—and screaming, lost hold of my bubble.

Thank God for the safety rope!

I plunged down—then jerked almost to a stop. Since I was attached to my uncle, it was as if a horse he was riding had suddenly reared up and gone staggering backward down a hill, very fast. He shouted, somehow still hanging on as he and his bubble reeled away, tilted bubble-up, with me

swinging along below, heels over head. The gardening shears went flying somewhere.

This is what happened in the first short moments of our practice flight. Picture it if you can!

The rest of the flight consisted of my *in loco parentis* and me and our single Knichtbubel bubble zooming along in this awkward way, on down toward the roofs of Mt. Geranium. There in the moonlight—but actually, there was no fine old friendly moonlight.

No moon.

If you went out in your backyard that moonless evening, and you happened to look up, I doubt you'd have known what to think of the strange big thingamajig you saw sailing by under the early stars. Or heard sailing by, since both me and my uncle were yelling at the top of our lungs.

I could actually make out Uncle Dudley's voice shouting, *"Hang on, Duncan lad, now hang on!"* For which I was grateful to him, I have to say.

He could easily have been screaming terrible curses, like other people in his situation might.

I don't have clear memories of the landscape that passed below, because of my upside-down position and the darkness, and the helmet slipping over my gaping eyes even then. Also a couple of pigeons had hitched on for a ride, out of curiosity. But I do recall the familiar look of a neighborhood, with a lot of pale bricks and cement driveways.

All of a sudden I heard Uncle Dudley squawking, *"Ready to land, Duncan! Ready to——"* and a chainlink fence flashed under me, and with a nasty crack on my head I crashed down onto something and stopped and then my uncle crashed violently on top of me.

And our Knichtbubel geranium joy ride was over!

"Wh—where are we?" I mumbled, flapping woozily.

We were on a picnic table.

"By the twelve charms of Zanzibar, we're on a picnic table!" announced Uncle Dudley, sitting up shakily, bubble-less and geranium-less. "Seem to be in a backyard. Oddly familiar. By a barbec—" His voice sounded hollow. *"Surely this can't be—"*

But it was.

An ungrateful hitchhiker pigeon emphasized the point by squirting him on the head as it flapped away.

Stu Bunkmeier (yes, that's whose backyard we'd landed in) insisted on driving us home. I sat grim and squashed in my safety pillows against the door, with a bag of ice from Dot for my goose egg

despite the helmet. Uncle Dudley stared stiffly ahead through the windshield. He'd done a lot of stammering when the bold *D* on his pigeon-dirtied handkerchief was noticed. It stood for *Derring-do,* he'd at last announced.

Sure. Right.

He flinched slightly every time Stu grinned over and snickered, *"Con-gee-gee!"* all the way to Clover Crescent.

Stu Bunkmeier was a truly evil man, I decided. As if I needed further evidence.

But what about Uncle Dudley?

Looking at him there, in his stuffed tweed and rabbit-ears handkerchief, I suddenly thought he seemed very . . . foolish. Dopey.

Even idiotic!

For the first time, doubts began to creep in about my uncle's marvelous abilities.

I felt miserable. My goose egg throbbed.

At Clover Crescent, more commotion was waiting, from a different Uncle Dudley "scientific practice." My uncle had sprinkled another of Knichtbubel Inst.'s select powders on the front of our house that afternoon, to test its "attractive power" on glowworms. The glowworms would spell out

WELCOME HOME, PECKLES!

in the night. It was to be another surprise for my parents.

The powder had proved so attractive that the blazing glowworms were visible half a mile away. A keen-eyed young reporter from the *Geranium Gazette* showed up to take pictures. Against his deepest desires, my uncle desperately pleaded to keep the Peckle name out of the paper. He was backed up by the nods and puffs of Mr. Adamzicki, who'd come along very slowly to see how we'd made out.

But the young reporter knew another front-page story when he saw one. Two pillowed Peckles in a fine stew!

Thank God at least Arthur wasn't around to gawk and cackle.

No, but he might as well have been.

CHAPTER SEVEN
clay feet

An air of gloom descended over Clover Crescent.

Even for an old pro at shrugging off disasters with a wink like Uncle Dudley, our great bubble fiasco was a terrible jolt. He didn't wink much the next day. Or the next.

Well, he did once, out of habit, when the *Gazette* with its photo scoop of us sat there on the kitchen table after I'd brought it in. (My parents were still on their road trip . . . as if under a Feathergold spell.) This was my first time ever seeing myself in the paper. I couldn't help a smile of pride, despite my own gloomy mood. A faint halfhearted wink came back at me—almost a wince, really. Delivered by a glum figure in a stained satin robe and ratty Panama hat. Hardly the picture of the hero he'd been to me, this uncle Dudley.

Mostly he kept away up on the third floor, and brooded. He took a break from that by wandering around under the maple tree in back, pulling at his goatee in a cloud of pipe smoke. Into which a glass of milk-and-rum punch would blur as he sipped.

My uncle's confidence was shaken, obviously. He must have felt his "inspired scheme" for Dot Bunkmeier's heart had been not only rejected, but *jeered at,* by fate. "A hard thing for a man with a poetic spirit and magical ambitions," I heard him murmur to himself, as he opened the fridge to refill his glass. Even for a man of the world supposedly, like Uncle Dudley.

And maybe too my uncle was depressed at what a lousy *in loco parentis* he was being. Maybe you wouldn't expect me to say this. But an adult in charge isn't supposed to act more irresponsibly than a kid, is he? I mean, it's unsettling. Grownups are supposed to be the safe and sensible ones, aren't they? Uncle Dudley just lifted his head glumly now and sighed, "Ah Duncan, Duncan lad . . ." when I lamely suggested "More midair practice?" over our TV-tray turkey.

Uncle Dudley sighed so much now, it was disconcerting.

To be honest, I'd figured I'd probably get nowhere on the bubble-practice topic.

To be even more honest, I can't say I really wanted to! I'd lost much of my appetite for Knichtbubel marvels. And flight. And surprising my parents at their motel. It was all Uncle Dudley's doing. Him and his disasters.

Because that's just what they were, I saw now.

The disappearing spells . . . the goblin cookies . . . the airborne flower scheme. I added up all my uncle's magical "Feathergoldian researches," and they all, one way or another, came to screwups! The falling pieces of a hero's clay feet. (When you thought your hero was made of solid gold.) What did I have to show for them? Okay, there was the gruesome thrill of Señor Recuerdo upstairs, but that was different. So what else?

My goose-egg bump on my head, that's what.

This goose egg came up for discussion at Gumberry Creek, where I'd resumed salvage operations with Arthur. Even flying along on a bicycle, you see, *"Hiyo!"*-ing, had lost its charms. Wallowing for hours in Gumberry's muddy shallows — that seemed suddenly very appealing again.

Then the photograph appeared in the *Gazette*. And Arthur pointed out with a sneer that my goose egg was visible in it.

"So?" I replied.

"So it makes you look even more idiotic," he said. Unaware of how he looked in his snorkel mask and nose clips.

"Oh yeah?" I responded. In defense of my goose egg.

We were conducting our conversation while draped over opposite sides of our Salvage Corp. inner tube.

"Sure," said Arthur. "Those dopey outfits in the photo, what could possibly make anybody dress up like that!"

"*Something* . . ." I informed him, mysteriously and aloofly.

"Oh yeah, what?"

I shrugged.

"He's a weirdo," sneered Arthur.

"Who?" I demanded.

"Your uncle."

"*Oh yeah?*" I replied, stung by the insult to our family honor, even if I was suffering similar doubts about Uncle Dudley myself. I jammed the inner tube into Arthur's chest.

"Everybody," Arthur gulped, "says so. That old tweed coat and hat, he looks like a bum — he's *idiotic!*" He jammed the inner tube into my chest.

I slapped water in his face. "*Who* says!"

"Everybody!" Arthur coughed. He slapped water back at me. "Mr. Feeley. Mr. Forrestal from the lumberyard!" (They were friends of Arthur's father from Walrus Club meetings.) Arthur laughed. "My dad says Mr. Forrestal says your uncle's got a crush on Dot Bunkmeier, it's *pathetic!*"

"*He does not!*" I snarled. I kicked him underwater. "*Take it back!*"

"Ow—does!" snarled Arthur, kicking in return.

"*Does not!*" I snarled again, lurching off-balance, then furiously water-slapping plus kicking.

At this point a halting voice called out my name. We both stopped and turned, panting and dripping, toward the bank.

"Duncan?" repeated Linda Cooch. She was tilting her head to peer at me, to make certain it was me—so that a layer of her golden hair hung down from her sun hat as if on display.

I blushed in shock. I admit it. She had on Bermuda shorts and a sky blue T-shirt. "Hi—Miss Cooch—" I gulped.

There was an awkward pause. "I didn't mean to interrupt you and your friend," she said softly. And she swallowed, and grinned, oddly. I blushed again. I felt a strange deep, fuzzy tingle. "It's—" I was interrupted by a sudden monkey laugh and a slap of water. *"Cut it out!*—" I hissed at Arthur and slapped back furiously.

This degenerated into a fit of both of us hacking away. By the time we were done, Linda Cooch was down at the bend in the path, disappearing.

That was all the chance meeting lasted. Who'd have thought it'd be the cause of so much trouble to come?

"She's *idiotic,*" Arthur sneered (though he blushed as he said it). This led to an exchange of arm punches. I stormed out of the water onto the bank.

Uncle Dudley's name came up again. "He's a *world voyager!*" I proclaimed grandly while toweling.

There was a baffled pause. Then Arthur cackled.

"Listen, Uncle Dudley's been all over, the most amazing places!" I went on.

"Yeah—like *Valparaíso!*" sneered Arthur.

The sheer arrogance of his tone was what led me to commit my act of irresponsibility next.

"Uncle Dudley is practically a *sorcerer!*" I blurted out, fiercely and triumphantly (and as much to impress myself really as Arthur). "He has potions and stuff, up in his room—he can do things, you just wouldn't believe it!"

Arthur's face changed—and I knew I'd spoken too much. He waded closer.

"What kind of potions and stuff?" he said. His voice was suddenly low and serious.

I shrugged, and rubbed my arm where he'd hit me. "Potions," I sniffed. "Stuff." I quickly put on my sneakers.

He repeated his question, but I stuck to my answer, despite his punching me again. He kept on demanding information, even when I ran off, leaving him to tie up the inner tube for the night by himself. He stood shivering on the bank in his swim trunks and snorkel, yelling after me.

But this scene with Arthur left my mind right after I arrived home. Something unexpected was waiting for me. A package, addressed very officially to "Mr. Duncan Peckle." A heavy package . . . from Cincinnati, Ohio.

My mother had sent it, from the road, to keep her telephone promise. Inside were three glass jars.

Supper that evening on Clover Crescent featured the curious flavors of chili sauce with chocolate.

"Yuck," I declared again, at the sight of it, as I had at my mother's original mention of it. But I actually had no problem finishing my portion, served over our quick-and-deluxe fish sticks. I had seconds even. Thirds.

"Yes, *peculiar* combination . . ." Uncle Dudley murmured glumly, as he clanked around with a tablespoon for the last chocolaty smears at the bottom of the first jar. As always, his appetite was immense, no matter what. "But *unexpectedly beguiling . . .*" he added.

Did a weak gleam flicker in his dull eyes as he licked the spoon clean?

Maybe, but I missed it. I was preoccupied with how ratty my uncle's Panama was, perched as ever on his head.

The chili-chocolate sauce reminded Uncle Dudley of a feast he'd had on a cocoa plantation, when he'd "roamed a season in pursuit of fortune, down there Sumatra way."

("Near *Valparaíso?*" piped Arthur's mean voice in my head.)

"Host, an Italian fella," my uncle went on, to me and Mr. Adamzicki now too, as we three sputtered along later in the station wagon toward the movie at the drive-in. "Great pride in his spaghetti, naturally, even thousands of miles from home."

Uncle Dudley had been guest of honor (so he said) at this spaghetti feast, in appreciation of his talent with a song. He cleared his throat to sing:

"Away away, in far Cathay,
Where the boats sail on the water,
I played each day with a fairy child,
Who was my master's daughter . . ."

Uncle Dudley wiped an eye with a knuckle and sighed deeply over the rumbling of the muffler.

Like I said, he could get emotional. But really, it was embarrassing now!

Mr. Adamzicki reached over and patted Uncle Dudley on the shoulder. And sighed himself.

"Affecting little verse," my uncle muttered with a sniff, feeling his sleeve over his tattoo.

Thanks to Mr. Adamzicki's driving, the sci-fi feature had of course already started by the time we pulled into our space at the drive-in, muffler growling. Our neighbors gave us a look.

They started to glare and "shush!" when Uncle Dudley couldn't stop the in-car speakers from playing at shrieking volume for several minutes. Then someone in the next row got out of his car and threatened to walk over when Mr. Adamzicki's horn began to beep all by itself. And only stopped when Mr. Adamzicki and Uncle

Dudley punched at the steering wheel furiously and then both grabbed it and shook it with all their might.

It was like bubble-launching all over again.

I sank low in the back seat, squirming in uncle-embarrassment. Was there anything, I thought, that Uncle Dudley could do normally and properly?

I squirmed more later, but for a different tingly reason, as I waved away the smoke from two pipes to clear a view through the windshield. Under the stars, the drive-in screen shone gigantically above us . . . and one giant head, belonging to the beautiful daughter of the movie's tragic hero, glowed especially. Because of her giant hair. Her long and flat and golden hair.

Just like Linda Cooch's . . .

I tingled. Just like I had in Gumberry Creek.

On the way home, Uncle Dudley and Mr. Adamzicki analyzed the themes of the movie. Meaning Mr. Adamzicki puffed away without a word as usual, while my uncle yacked on for the both of them.

"Noblest ambition!" insisted Uncle Dudley. "*That's* what inspired that scientific genius, Prof. O'Hardwich, to experiment with his elixir-potion for universal love!"

Was there a hint now of my uncle's old enthusiastic spirit? "An elixir for love!" my uncle repeated, almost to himself. Almost as if the drama of Prof. O'Hardwich was somehow his own.

Was it really the noble scientist's fault, Uncle Dudley suddenly pleaded, that a slight miscalculation in his elixir researches created a horde of giant spiders that terrorized the town?

My uncle laughed, and waved a bony fist—in actual high spirits! He looked around at me. "That would be something, Duncan, eh? A horde of giant spiders, here in sleepy old Mt. Geranium!" And he winked. Just like the Uncle Dudley of old.

And you know what? I have to admit it. I winked back.

Not right away, and only a slight wink. But a wink. I even grinned. Not a big grin, hardly. But a grin nevertheless, despite the remains of my goose egg. It was hard to resist Uncle Dudley, back at his old Dudley self.

But that's not the full story. Not at all. My admiration for my uncle didn't resume just like that. No. I'd been struck by inspiration.

A marvelous inspiration!

I was developing a scheme . . . a scheme of inspired cunning!

"Spiders . . ." mumbled Mr. Adamzicki faintly through his pipe. And he shuddered.

Naturally, considering who was driving the car and who was navigating, we got lost. After wandering for an hour in a maze of unfamiliar dark shady lanes, Uncle Dudley spotted a porch where two figures sat by a kerosene lamp. He hopped out while we waited at the corner, our muffler rumbling.

"Ahoy there, my good——" we heard my uncle begin, at a white front gate. Then a blood-curdling bestial roar drowned him out, and he came hurtling back toward us with a furious black Doberman behind him. He slammed the door on its snarling jaws, just before they could chomp on his "personal particulars," as he put it with a breathless laugh when we were safely around the corner.

"By the hairs of Attila's hound," he whooped, "reminds me of an incident once with a guard's mastiff—there under the sickle moon of Peshawar town!"

Yes, he was back, all right, my uncle Dudley of old.

And I won't pretend I wasn't glad to see him. He was much better than the glum, depressed Uncle Dudley any day. I didn't care how Arthur might sneer. Because I had a scheme to turn everything right!

Eventually we found Clover Crescent, thanks to a Mt. Geranium police car that heard our muffler, and gave Mr. Adamzicki directions, along with a ticket for being a public nuisance.

Lying waiting for sleep, I thought of the movie again—and its elixir of love. I didn't think of Prof. O'Hardwich, though. I thought of

Rudolph, his keen-eyed young assistant. As if Rudolph's story were my own! Rudolph—whose brilliant intervention supplied the antidote to which the giant spiders eventually succumbed. Rudolph—who corrected the Professor's mistake in his great elixir research too, humbly!

These thoughts of love elixirs might have led me to thoughts of golden-haired Linda Cooch. But like I say, I was shy.

Instead I conjured up how Dot Bunkmeier would develop a crush on Uncle Dudley—a huge crush that would absolutely humiliate Arthur and his fellow critics, evil Stu Bunkmeier, fat Mr. Feeley, and the others. The bunch of them.

Uncle Dudley was a pretty curious and marvelous person, yes he was. At least he had it in him to be. A kind of wizard almost, or close enough. His strange clothes were *strange*, weren't they? No one *ordinary* would dress like that. So what if he got his geography mixed up at times? And needed some help with his Knichtbubel schemes and researches? And wasn't a perfect *in loco parentis*?

Because I, Duncan Peckle, would help him! I'd already rescued him once before, during the disappearing spells episode, hadn't I? Of course.

I would be my uncle Dudley's Rudolph!

"An elixir of love . . ." I murmured, cunningly, half-asleep.

I'd forgotten all about my irresponsible remarks to Arthur that afternoon, regarding the "stuff" up in Uncle Dudley's room. . . .

Little did I know that a mile and a half away, Arthur lay in bed thinking about my irresponsible remarks that afternoon regarding the "stuff" in Uncle Dudley's room. And he thought again, as he had all evening, about Linda Cooch

in her sky blue T-shirt. *"Idiotic,"* he mumbled. And he squirmed, and tingled. He wasn't quite as shy as I was, though. "A love potion," he whispered. *"An exclixer of love . . ."* he added, mispronouncing the word because he'd only read it a few hours before in his family's encyclopedia, under 'Potions.'. . .

Little did I know that up on the third floor, Uncle Dudley was whispering to himself: "An elixir of love!" The old gleam burned again in his eyes as he hunted through his boxes and packets of Knichtbubel products. Finally he found what he wanted: and he dipped two fingers first into one particular box and then into one particular packet, and then he rubbed the wick of a candle between them. He turned off the bed lamp and lit the treated candle and held it near the open window.

A brief pause . . . then a sudden *whump!*—and the window screen actually bulged inward, fuzzy and fluttering, as a horde of flame-crazy moths tried to burst in.

My uncle nodded and blew out the candle. *"An elixir of love . . ."* he whispered again. And he smiled in the darkness under his Panama hat.

Downstairs I smiled on my sleepy pillow.

About a mile and a half away, dreaming Arthur smiled too.

I'm not sure about Mr. Adamzicki. Maybe he knew better. But the other three of us were all smiling, that Mt. Geranium summer night.

Next night would be very different.

I was about to make sure of that.

CHAPTER EIGHT
elixirs everywhere

Uncle Dudley was whistling when he came clomping downstairs in the morning. Very late in the morning, of course. Whistling and in a fine mood; he already had on his tweed and his Panama.

"Ah, Duncan, my fine twig off the old family branch!" he declared. "What a glorious summer day to be alive, eh, lad?"

Then he yawned, because he'd stayed up very late. And he invited me to join him, "To sample the sweet Mt. Geranium air on an invigorating ramble to collegiate greenswards!" Meaning a nice walk to the college campus. It was always a bit hard to follow my uncle when he got talking in his fancy storybook way.

I was delighted by the invite, just like old times. I could barely believe my luck. "That'd be great," I said. Then I swallowed hard, trying to look glum. "But I gotta stay here . . . and . . . and do something. For my mom," I stammered.

It was the first time I'd ever told a proper scheming lie to a grownup. My heart beat noisily and I was afraid my cheeks were red.

But Uncle Dudley just put his hand on my shoulder and sighed down at me in admiration, and said if only he'd been half as virtuous at my age as I was!

I spied through the window, as he rambled away down Clover Crescent. When his Panama was out of sight, I turned slowly and swallowed hard again. And then I raced into the kitchen for a cup and shot up to the third floor like lightning.

The guest room was as cluttered as when I'd seen it before. Even more cluttered. It was probably

the messiest room I'd ever been in! You could tell
a wizard type did his researches here—and that
he was very disorganized. How right, that I'd
decided to help him.

Stealthily I began poking around, while Señor
Recuerdo's dark little face glared at me from
under a sock on the card table. More crumpled

socks covered the higgledy-piggledy Knichtbubel boxes and packets and jars. Dr. Feathergold, I discovered, offered hair-care products to his subscribers, besides everything else. I found a tube of DYNAMIZED DANDRUFF DEACTIVATOR and a square purple box of glittering crystals, labeled HAIR REJUVENATOR FOR THE DISTINGUISHED ALCHEMIST—DK BROWN. Then I found some GENERAL PURPOSE TOAD WITCHING POWDER, and some SPECIAL PURPOSE TOAD GRIT, FOR FERRIC-AUREATIC CONVERSION (meaning that it changed iron into gold). Then a jar of our bubble-compound mix, which I started to open, just to—when the floor creaked outside!

I spun around. Not breathing, heart hammering. Silence.

"Hello?" I called faintly.

I crept to the door, and opened it a crack. No one.

The scare got me moving furiously. It took nerves of steel, I could see, to be another Rudolph coming to the aid of a great but unorganized mind. Beneath a pair of checked green socks, I spotted at last what I was after—a packet inked with a big question mark:

?

that had been scratched out, and:

eliXir/ L⁰Ve!!

added instead!

With a trembly hand I shook some elixir powder into my cup, then stuffed the packet back under the socks as if nothing had been touched, and dusted away powder I'd shakily spilled. Then

I crept to the door, and checked—and then scurried back down to the safety of my room. Done!

A big grin spread over my face as I carefully stirred the elixir into the jar of Cincinnati chili-chocolate sauce on my desk. Maybe I wouldn't have grinned quite so wide if I'd stopped to think that since Uncle Dudley's room was so disorganized, the contents of each box or packet might not always agree with its label.

But I was new at being a wizardly assistant, so I wasn't as careful as I could have been. I almost licked the delicious spoon, in fact, until I remembered at the last second. I wrapped it in some old construction paper along with the cup, then hid spoon and cup under my bed. After this I washed my hands very thoroughly. That I did proudly remember to do.

After which I got on my bike, and with Uncle Dudley still away on his ramble, I sped off toward Geranium center with the jar of elixirized sauce.

"Why, Duncan, what a neat surprise!" said Dot, as I came panting in to Kefauver's lunch counter. Only one other customer was there, old

Mr. Feldstein in his fishing cap, eating a bowl of vegetable soup, which was *his* usual.

"Thought you and your uncle had forgotten all about me!" Dot went on cheerily. "Where you gents been? All on your own today?"

I explained that Uncle Dudley was on his ramble—that we'd been "you know, very busy and all." And with my heart hammering, I placed the jar of sauce on the counter. I swallowed

and explained that I wasn't having lunch. I was delivering a gift from Uncle Dudley:

"A special, secret gift."

I hardly stammered at this point. Maybe I was improving as a liar. I mean, a schemer.

"'A special, secret gift,'" repeated Dot, and she blinked, and laughed. Old Mr. Feldstein looked over and did something he always did with his false teeth with his mouth closed.

"It's for you alone to eat," I instructed. "It's chili-chocolate sauce from Cincinnati—it's *delicious!*"

"Well, I bet it is!" Dot grinned.

I leaned over closer. "Uncle Dudley really wants to know how you like it," I murmured. "He says—he says you should eat it—*tonight!* And . . . *think of him?* He'll come here. *Tomorrow!*"

There was a funny pause as Dot stared down at me. Then suddenly she laughed, loud, and slapped the counter.

"Why, I'll be delighted!" she declared cheerily. "The pair of you two!" she added, shaking her head. She picked up the jar and gave it a wiggle. "Tonight? You betcha! And you say thanks to your Uncle Dudley there, okay!" She ruffled my hair. "So how's ole 'Hiyo' Harry these days, anyway?"

"Hiyo" Harry was *kid stuff*, I thought as I pedaled away from town center. Because I was a real-life Rudolph, like in the movie! Performing actual Knichtbubel Inst. wizardry, despite my young age. Pretty brilliant, you'd have to admit. Not too bad for a shy kid! Magic wasn't hardly so hard, it turned out (at least for me). But I felt modest too, like Rudolph, at the same time.

I wanted someone to gloat to, and I headed for Arthur's house. I wouldn't let out any details, of course. I'd just quietly grin and gloat.

But Arthur wasn't home, said his father. So I headed back to Clover Crescent, grinning anyway in the summer sunshine. Just may-be wishing Rudolph had a somewhat different name. I was whistling, in fact, when I turned our corner.

And was startled to see someone hurrying from our front door and down the front steps and picking his bicycle off the ground.

Arthur?

He almost jumped when I shouted, twisting around with a strange alarmed look. Then he leaped on his bike. "Gotta get back . . . help my dad . . . with chores!" he cried over his shoulder, pedaling frantically away.

"*Wait!*" I yelled, and was just about to go after him when I heard, "Ahoy there, Duncan!" behind me. Uncle Dudley came marching along hurriedly from his ramble. He'd just remembered that Mr. Adamzicki was coming over to take him to a "luncheon musicale." I only got a puzzling glimpse of Arthur, disappearing around the corner, before the thunder of a muffler filled Clover Crescent and Mr. Adamzicki's station wagon came growling up. To take Uncle Dudley, characteristically, straight back where he'd just come from: the college, where the lunch concert was going to be.

While Uncle Dudley freshened up inside, I spent the next ten minutes crawling under the station wagon in search of the little expensive thing that was supposed to stop the muffler from making noise.

Had I been able to chase Arthur around the corner, this is what I'd have seen: Arthur letting out a yelp—and floating straight up high in the air off his bike seat, and then floating down, and losing his balance, and going sprawling.

And giggling as he looked back around and hopped back on, and went pedaling madly away again.

Arthur had snuck up to the third-floor guest room himself, I'd find out later. He'd given the taste-test to the packet of bubble-compound mix, out of curiosity. He liked it! Then he'd almost jumped out of his skin at the sight of Señor Recuerdo scowling at him.

He also thought he found what he was after, a tube of FOLLICULAR ATTRACTION POTION. He didn't know it wasn't love elixir, just gel my uncle rubbed in his hair to keep from going bald.

But I knew nothing about all this right then. I felt puzzled that Arthur had been nosing around, but I was sure he wouldn't *dare* go up to my uncle's room.

Mainly I was impatient for the hours to pass until dinner, at which time Dot would eat the elix-irized chili sauce—and true researched wizardry would take place! Tomorrow I'd lead Uncle

Dudley to Kefauver's for lunch, to witness my cunning scheme's success. How could Rudolph have done better?

But it was tough, just waiting for everything to happen. *Being patient.* It wore on your nerves, this wizard stuff.

I wandered along Gumberry Creek to get my mind off things, stopping at the Salvage Corp. inner tube, tied to its tree by the bank. I hung around and ate some blackberries off a bush and redid the tie-up and skipped stones on the water. I kept looking back down the path to see if Linda Cooch was coming. Like yesterday afternoon. I realized I was hoping she would, that's why I was there. My heart began to hammer and hammer. And I became more and more relieved, I admit, when she didn't appear. When I finally started back down the path home, I hurried, hoping now that I *wouldn't* run into her!

Confusing? It was some kind of day, all right.

Uncle Dudley was just back from his concert when I arrived at Clover Crescent. He was in the kitchen, giving his hands a soapy scrub. *"Tsk tsk,"* he said, with a grin. "Can't be too careful about spreading Feathergold matter by accident!" And he winked. He was still in fine spirits. The college musicale had been *"Bravissimo!"* he declared (meaning terrific). "Talented young ladies. Exemplary refreshments."

We went out into the backyard and sat in the twilight just like we used to, me with my iced tea, Uncle Dudley with his milk punch. He hummed some of the tunes from the musicale and demonstrated how impressively the college violinist had played. Then he lit his pipe and nodded contentedly at me.

"*Tomorrow*, young Duncan, that's the heart's big day," he declared, with a dreamy kind of look. "When Feathergold's elixir of love goes to conquer at Kefauver's lunch counter!"

For a moment I just gawked at him, thinking he knew about my secret scheme. Then he went on about his "ardent researches into a love potion — *shh!* — perfected with a last final adjustment this very morning." He grinned and put a bony finger to his goateed lips and said, *"Ssh!"*

again, as if this was *his* big secret. I was way ahead of him! I put a finger to my own lips and said, "*Ssh!*" too, and grinned—for my own reasons.

You could easily conclude that I was a better wizard than my uncle.

For supper we had Salisbury steak dinners,

saving the chili-chocolate sauce for tomorrow to draw out the pleasure. I had a story prepared in case Uncle Dudley wondered why there was only one jar left. It was like old happy times again, before the bubble fiasco. And I was thinking to myself of Dot sampling the elixirized sauce, probably that very moment—

When we heard a loud thumping at the front door.

And then a female voice called, *"Yoo-hoo!"* very strangely from outside.

I blinked at Uncle Dudley. Uncle Dudley blinked at me. Together we got up and approached the front door, and opened it carefully, and peered out into the dimness. There was no one in sight. A huge bouquet of roses lay on the welcome mat. With a note. Uncle Dudley picked up the note, and we both stared at the handwriting.

"*'To the Handsomest Man in the Whole World,'*" Uncle Dudley read aloud.

We looked at each other in bewilderment. Giggles came suddenly from the other side of the porch. And up the front steps leaped—Linda Cooch!

A hardly recognizable Linda Cooch! Linda Cooch in lipstick and a super-short shiny red dress and weird black stockings like fishnet, with her golden hair all pulled over to one side of her head.

"*Oh darling, my darling!*" she cried, throwing her arms around Uncle Dudley and covering his face with smooching kisses! Her eyes glowed red like a demon's under their dark lashes.

My uncle struggled and managed to get himself free, and he jumped inside. I did too, just before he slammed the door and turned the lock.

We gaped at each other as scratching and cooing and thumping kept on at the door.

"By the seven pillows of the Sultan's harem!" panted Uncle Dudley, his face covered in lipstick. "I believe it's the cello player from the musicale."

I squawked that I knew who she was—*she was my cello teacher!*

Uncle Dudley blinked and then stared down at his fingernails—and slapped his forehead under his Panama.

"Did I shake her hand to congratulate her this afternoon, with my elixir-begrimed fingernails?" he cried.

In a sickening flash I realized what had happened. It was another Knichtbubel "complication." The latest Uncle Dudley disaster. My uncle had accidentally infected *Linda Cooch* with his love elixir!

It was too much.

After all my efforts to help him, Uncle Dudley had shown how hopeless and incompetent a wizard—or whatever you want to call it—he was! What a *jerk!* I felt disgusted. Betrayed. Humiliated. Furious.

"Duncan lad, whither goest?" he cried, as I rushed stomping up the stairs. "Courage, nephew, remember Horatio at the bridge!—" he began, but had to turn back to the door, where Linda Cooch's thumping and cooing had grown frantic. "Now now, miss," I heard him call. "Now there, now now!"

I locked myself in my room and just sat on the bed in the dark, staring at nothing, beside myself. Soon Uncle Dudley came knocking at the door, very concerned, wanting to know what was wrong.

What was wrong? Everything about him! "Go away, Uncle Dudley!" I yelled. And he did.

And I just sat and stared, maybe sniffing, I admit, thinking how horrible and embarrassing my summer had become.

And that's when I had my real inspiration.

Just like that, I knew what to do. Forget being another Rudolph, forget stupid Knichtbubel "researches," forget—all of it! I figured out something simple and unmagical and just right—what kids in my situation have always done, when life becomes intolerable.

I peered out my window. I could hear Uncle Dudley's lame voice trying to be calm at the front door below. Linda Cooch had climbed up into the big shade tree by the curb. She was serenading my uncle, blowing kisses to him, her eyes glowing red. Linda Cooch!

I turned bitterly, dug around in the closet for my old backpack, and then crept out of my room, and downstairs—sneaking through the hall behind Uncle Dudley, who stood out on the welcome mat, pleading. In the kitchen I stuck the last jar of chili-chocolate sauce in my backpack, for nourishment, and then crept out the back door and got my bike. Stealthily I wheeled it down the driveway in the shadows of the bushes. Then I jumped on—

And I ran away from home, into the Mt. Geranium night.

CHAPTER NINE
running away

I rushed up dark leafy streets, under the crescent moon. Where to, I had no idea. Just as far away from my hateful uncle as I could get, from the atrocious sight of his atrocious magic with Linda Cooch.

The whole world seemed strange and eerie as I raced along. Strange dogs barked from porches. The slice of moon went in and out of clouds. Speeding around a corner, I saw two dark figures weirdly prancing along the sidewalk in the distance—singing. They had on top hats and capes, as if in costume for Halloween even though it was summer. I saw them hop over a fence onto a lawn, prancing and singing, and start tearing up flower beds!

Eerie. *Strange.* I shot past—neither seeing their red-glowing eyes right then, nor being aware who they were. For a second I thought I recognized Mr. Feeley's voice, and Stu Bunkmeier's! But how absurd was that?

And I didn't care; all I cared about was pedaling on, harder and harder, farther and farther away from my atrocious uncle!

Until I was somewhere on the outskirts of Mt. Geranium, where nothing looked familiar at all. I was panting and sweating and my legs were aching. Long shadows loomed. I couldn't see any houses, just wide lonely fields, and giant, dark, scary oaks. Suddenly a savage barking erupted behind me. I tore along wildly, my heart racing. The barking drifted away. I slowed, gulping, and then a rush of wings brushed my head—a *bat!* I swerved, and went careening out of control off the road into a field. And crashed.

A bad crash.

I lay in the prickly grass, groaning. My right ankle throbbed. I felt a big lump on my head—another goose egg. Very groggily I became aware of the light of a small fire somewhere nearby. And then little voices. Then little figures, hurrying over. Little scowling faces with big pointy ears, staring down at me.

CHAPTER TEN
Bump's domain

I had crashed in Farmer Swenson's field, it turned out, among a pack of goblins who were all tipsy and ornery from the lactose in a carton of chocolate milk they'd gotten hold of. They crowded around me now, not looking cute at all. Because I was so dazed and couldn't move because of my ankle, I protested only feebly when many little scavenging hands snatched off my backpack. Right away they had the jar of chili-chocolate sauce out, and were prying at the lid.

"Yes, okay, go ahead and try the sauce," I mumbled, trying to sound gracious and assured as they struggled with the lid. I'd read somewhere that was the best way to act in potentially hostile situations. "But please help me," I added woozily. "Where's my bike?" I blinked, looking around hopefully for two familiar goblin faces.

"Where are you going?" demanded a skinny little fellow with unpleasant foxy features. He swayed forward in a funny high collar and funny high boots.

I don't know why I answered, but I did. "I'm running away from home," I declared. "From my uncle, I mean."

"Why? What's he done? Who are you?"

"He's . . . well, never mind. I'm Duncan Peckle of Clover Crescent. Who are you?" I demanded back. My head hurt, and my eyes just wouldn't seem to focus.

"You watch your tone!" snapped the skinny fellow, stamping a boot.

"Why, it's young kind sir!" slurred a female voice. My old backyard guest, Hettie Buckle, lurched close, blinking. "Look, Abe!"

Abe Basket with his torn ear appeared beside her. He wobbled, tipsy and bad-tempered as when I'd last seen him. "You . . ." he muttered slowly. "With the *terrier!* . . ." There were gasps and snarls around me. I protested Abe's awful memory.

Shouts drowned us out—the lid of the jar was off. The skinny fellow demanded first taste. Dramatically he reached a finger in, scowled, and tasted while everyone else looked on.

"Better than chocolate milk," he announced, with a nod and a hiccup. "*Peculiar* combination, but *unexpectedly beguiling!*" The others swarmed over the jar.

I watched in alarm. "Gee, I sure hope there isn't tons of lactose in that chocolate sauce," I murmured. The evidence of Uncle Dudley's warning about the effects of lactose on goblins was already all around me. The skinny fellow whirled around.

"What's wrong with lactose?" he demanded.

"Nothing," I stammered. "It's just, my uncle warned, I mean told me . . . 'cause you've already had chocolate milk, you see. But I don't think chocolate *sauce* has it . . . unless it's *milk* choco—"

"You don't think? You don't think?" sputtered the skinny fellow. He hopped up and down in a fury with both boots, so his collar flew up past his ears. "Who are you, to come into honest Timothy Bump's domain, telling honest folk about lactose and what you don't think—eh? Eh?"

I apologized. But Timothy Bump wagged his finger. I needed a lesson, that's what—a lesson in manners!

"So he does," chimed in Abe Basket, wiping his chili-chocolaty lips with a burp. "On account of the *terrier!*"

"A lesson! A lesson!" cried Timothy Bump.

"But I'm sure he meant no harm," protested Hettie Buckle, who had chocolate sauce on her nose and braids. "He has a kind heart, a good kind heart!"

I apologized again, as sincerely as I could, concerned at how ugly things were getting. But then I accidently said "Mr. Bunk" as I asked again for help with my bike.

"What did you call me?!" snarled Timothy Bump. Truly hopping mad. Ferociously he ordered

me tied up—with stinkweed! "On account of the *terrier!*" Abe Basket hiccuped, as many grubby fierce little hands pinned me down.

I struggled, gnashing my teeth because of my ankle. No use.

Timothy Bump strode up and down. "A lesson, a lesson!" he chanted. All at once he whirled around. "We'll ransom him!" he cried. "That's it. He's run away from home, or his uncle, or whomever—we'll make 'em ransom him back!" He laughed. "Though they probably haven't missed such a rude, stupid boy," he sneered, "and don't care if he ever ever comes back!"

His cruel words pierced me deep as I shivered there all alone, captive of nasty scavengers in a cold dark field under the faraway splinter of moon.

That's what I'd got for trying to play the young wizard.

What would they ransom me for? *More chocolate sauce!* "But there's no more left," I protested.

"Oh, what an evil *lying* boy," Timothy Bump cried.

Abe Basket suggested bashing me with a rock,

and tottered off to look for one. Hettie Buckle tried to call him back. My feet were bound with stinkweed. "My ankle!" I yelped, and struggled helplessly again.

Hettie Buckle wailed and threw herself down messily on top of me to protect me. She was pulled off. "All right then!" she warned dramatically, with a hiccup. And she staggered slowly back, reciting some kind of spell in my defense. Timothy Bump laughed. So did everyone else. Hettie got confused and lost her place, and the goblins all laughed louder.

"You stop that!" I shouted at them—but when she tripped and sprawled on her back, and lay snoring, there was mean, drunken merriment all around.

Abe Basket came back with a rock. Room was cleared for him. The rock was lifted, drunkenly fumbled. Lifted again.

"You stop that, at once!" instructed a small bossy voice suddenly.

The goblins turned—then all shrank back. Three little personages strode up. They wore short velvet cloaks and leotards, and they were blond and almost too handsome, with golden curls and perfect posture. The Fairies from my *Chocklee's Encyclopedia!*

"Desist, ruffians—release this boy, begone!" piped the apparent leader, very nobly, nose in the air.

The goblins cowered and muttered and started to do as told. "Here, who are you?" demanded Timothy Bump, with a hiccup. The snooty blond leader announced that Timothy Bump knew perfectly well they were highborn fairies. Who were ordering their inferiors to halt

their drunken crimes! Timothy Bump hopped at
this insult, got a slap, kicked back at the fairy
leader—who then kicked him so hard right
between his legs that Timothy Bump flew out of
his boots.

The three fairies then started slapping and kicking all the goblins, who howled and ran off in chaos.

At this point there was the rumble of a muffler, and honking, and the flash of headlights, the crunch of tires on prickly grass. Uncle Dudley's voice called, "Are you all right, brave, beloved Duncan? *Savages!*" he shouted after the goblins.

He and Mr. Adamzicki half-carried me into the station wagon and loaded in my twisted bike, which they found by the goblins' fire. Then they thanked the highborn fairies, who by frantic researches my uncle had been able to summon to locate and rescue me. (They were superintelligent, and very stuck-up about it.) From the back seat, I woozily heard the noble little voices start to pipe in protest about something. Then Uncle Dudley jumped frantically into the seat beside me and Mr. Adamzicki roared us away, as scraps of cow patty smacked against our windows, and shocking curses from highborn voices stung our ears.

Apparently my uncle was supposed to pay the fairies for their aid with lemon custard. But naturally, on the way there, he and Mr. Adamzicki had found the custard too enticing not to try.

"It had gingersnap tidbits," Uncle Dudley explained. Mr. Adamzicki grunted at the memory.

And so, unfortunately, they'd finished it.

As Mr. Adamzicki drove to the hospital to get my ankle looked at, there was plenty of time to hear what had happened since I'd run away. I slumped in the seat, wrapped in a blanket, while Uncle Dudley patted my shoulder and informed me, clearing his throat, that Linda Cooch had climbed the maple in the backyard to blow kisses. Then had actually chased the station wagon down the street as it left!

"Cursed negligence," Uncle Dudley sighed. Guilty and distressed.

I kept a sullen face. I have to admit I was sort of grateful, and maybe even impressed by my rescue. But I wasn't letting my uncle know that — never mind his guilt and distress. Not right then, not with all the thoughtless damage he'd done—that he always seemed to do. And after all my inspired assistance!

But something remained very odd about things, I heard him brooding. The demonic red glow of Linda Cooch's eyes . . . *that* wouldn't derive from love elixir under fingernails. . . .

"More the effect of Perverse Metamorphic Compound," Uncle Dudley muttered. "Specially designed to spark the hidden naughty devil in whoever eats it. Appears to have infected George Feeley and Stu Bunkmeier too somehow! Passed 'em on the way out, " he informed me. "In top hats and capes, rampaging away with a song and dance in the flower beds!

"Feeley and *Bunkmeier* . . ." my uncle repeated, puzzling.

I had a slow, dreadful thought.

I blurted out a question.

Uncle Dudley shook his head. "No, no sign at all of beloved Dorothy." *But thinking it over,* he murmured that it seemed his Feathergold stocks had been fooled with! "As if someone had intruded into my chamber," he declared in disbelief, "and recklessly left about traces of their irresponsible mishandlings." Doubly reckless of them, because he had a habit of sometimes mislabeling his stocks.

My uncle looked down at his fingernails, shaking his head.

I shrank down under my blanket. So could all this chaos be partly because of me, and some unforeseen mistakes in my love-elixir scheme? Jeez, this wasn't how things had gone for brilliant young Rudolph! I guess magical doings weren't such a snap? I shivered and yawned, and wished I could fall asleep right away. And, if possible, never wake up.

"Which is why . . ." Uncle Dudley began, his voice dark and serious.

But just then Mr. Adamzicki jammed on the brakes, and we all lurched forward.

"Skunks," Mr. Adamzicki announced faintly, as a family of them crossed in our headlights. He hurried to roll up his window.

As I did the same, my sleepy eyes widened at the sight of something up in the trees by my side of the car.

Something unbelievable.

A boy was floating along, thirty feet in the air, giggling—apparently fast asleep! Tiny bubbles streamed from his mouth. He stayed in my view only a moment, before shooting away through the treetops on a gust of wind. I didn't blurt out his name, though I recognized his Gumberry Salvage Corp. T-shirt.

Because a wizardly assistant who's screwed up badly learns to keep very, very quiet.

"Which is why I've decided to take a momentous action . . ." Uncle Dudley continued, as at last we pulled up noisily to Florence Nightingale Hospital.

Besides all else, this night of misguided magic marked my first visit to a hospital emergency room. But I was disappointed. My ankle turned out to have been only badly twisted, not even a

sprain. Nothing grand at all. The doctor fixed me up with an Ace bandage and gave me a Band-Aid and an aspirin for my second goose egg, and he grinned as I almost fell asleep on his examining table. He suggested I spend my midnights in bed, not out wrecking my bike.

"Indeed," agreed my *in loco parentis.* "Indeed."

"Yes, a necessary momentous action," murmured Uncle Dudley, as we rumbled back at long last onto Clover Crescent, past trampled flower beds and mailboxes jammed with torn flowers and silly poems painted on parked cars. Stu Bunkmeier and Mr. Feeley must have had a fine old time.

As for floating Arthur, I don't know where he was right then. About forty miles away probably, asleep in midair. Probably mumbling, *"Idiotic,"* in his dreams.

As for Linda Cooch, thankfully she seemed to have gone to bed for the night.

CHAPTER ELEVEN
brave decision,
awesome visit

The problem, my uncle explained, was confusion in his Knichtbubel supplies. The third-floor guest room was always a mess, but it was a mess he knew well. "Now security's been breached, materials shifted and disturbed," he said. He couldn't trust himself to know exactly what was what, where was where now. And the risks were "too perilous and grave . . ."

"By the dreadful bogs of Machu Picchu," he added—whatever those were—stroking his goatee.

Our conversation took place the next afternoon in the living room at Clover Crescent. I had slept past lunchtime and now I sat with my wrapped-up ankle on my dad's footstool. Another lazy Mt. Geranium summer day. Hard to believe all the craziness of last night really happened.

But it did happen. I had my second goose egg to prove it.

Uncle Dudley had already had a "discreet confabulation" with Dot Bunkmeier down at Kefauver's, where he learned about my gift of chili-chocolate sauce, for which Dot thanked him heartily. She'd run out to the store while it was on the stove last night, and when she got back, "Bun-bun" and "Georgie" had already gobbled up every bit!

"Musta been *delicious*," she complimented my uncle. And why, yes, she had noticed a change in their behavior. And she "kinda liked the new Stu" she saw last night! She laughed. "I think that dressy style suits him." Stu was sleeping late today. The rascal! Probably planning another outing for tonight.

"A remarkable woman," Uncle Dudley sighed. "Remarkable."

At this point I mumbled my sheepish apology for ruining his own plans. I confessed how I'd wanted to be like young you-know-who in the movie. At which my uncle swallowed very hard and slowly rubbed his tattoo. And then apologized himself again for Linda Cooch, and for "any damage to higher affections for her." At which point I think I turned red.

"Very likely now she'll be back again tonight," he warned. "Love elixir's power enhanced by Metamorphic Compound." He'd got compound on his fingers, you see, when he rushed in yesterday to spruce up for the college musicale. Love elixir was already under his fingernails.

It was all one big wizardly mess.

"Bubble mix's been moved around too," he said.

I gulped, and in a small voice, made my Arthur confession too. I sure was doing a lot more confessing than magic-celebrating! My uncle gulped back, his eyes very wide.

"Well, well. Here we are," he said. "Two bungling peas in the same pod, uncle and nephew."

The day before, I would have sneered at this.

But not now.

"All the more reason for my momentous decision," Uncle Dudley declared, nodding solemnly.

This was his decision:

He had telephoned the great Dr. Julius Feathergold—personally—and as a subscriber, pleaded for his help.

The grand man was arriving in person at Clover Crescent, before dusk today! The floating-Arthur business would be one more "complication" for him to address.

I was stunned.

"Yes, Duncan lad, the blame's all mine," Uncle Dudley announced. "I'm the one who brought awesome Knichtbubel materials into this home. My prodigious burden.

"Oh, if I'd been by myself," he declared, "banging about the old globe, off Mayan shores or up Barbary highlands, I'd risk my chances!" (I wasn't sure about his geography, but I didn't complain.) "But now I see how I'm endangering you, beloved nephew. And that's intolerable. No matter how brave you are. No, I realize it now—*intolerable!*"

He pulled at his goatee in silence. Then he grinned weakly and murmured that calling Dr. Feathergold was a bad mark on a subscriber's reputation. It meant you weren't fully capable of handling Knichtbubel supplies and researches, and their awesome responsibility. He gave a feeble laugh. He looked pale.

Young as I was, I think I had a sense of the pain my uncle felt right then, as a voyager with wizardly ambitions.

"But no, I will not further endanger my brave favorite nephew!" he declared.

And I guess at that moment, my uncle Dudley grew up. Maybe it's strange for a kid to say that about an adult. But that's what I felt. I looked at my uncle with new eyes. Okay, he had some flaws as a magician. Who probably didn't? But he was as brave and caring an uncle as you could want! A true *in loco parentis.* He was sacrificing himself for my sake.

He was heeding family ties. From his heart.

I pleaded that we didn't need Dr. Feathergold, we could solve things ourselves, him and me! Hadn't we before, with the disappearing-spell ordeal?

But Uncle Dudley said no.

"By the crown on the monkey child's head"—whatever that meant—"no!" Only Dr. Feathergold could straighten everything out.

Dr. Feathergold himself!

I didn't argue more. I admit I was thrilled at the prospect of meeting the genius of the Knichtbubel Institute. *A real-life master wizard!*

Did he wear a long black coat and a high hat? Old-fashioned spectacles? Did he carry thick, dusty, ancient books? Like the wizard in *Chocklee's Encyclopedia*?

We spent the rest of the afternoon tidying the house for the great man's arrival. Mr. Adamzicki would be coming over too, once he got his car from the muffler repair shop; Uncle Dudley had told him everything. My uncle asked if there was any more chili-chocolate sauce to offer our honored guest. I apologized that the goblins had got the last of it. That was a true shame, my uncle muttered.

We waited. The shadows got longer and darker. Twilight began to fall. Where was Dr. Feathergold? Elixired and compounded Linda Cooch might show up again any minute! There was the rumble of a noisy muffler outside. Mr. Adamzicki? We peered out the front window. A hot rod had pulled up. A teenager got out, about the age of a high-school junior. His hair was long and slicked with grease, and he wore an ill-fitting leather jacket. He came toward our porch, squinting at a piece of paper, and climbed the steps. He knocked on our door.

"Yes?" said my uncle, opening the door a crack.

"Hey, what say?" said the teenager, grinning. "I'm Feathergold."

It was Dortmund Feathergold, grandnephew of the great genius. Dr. Feathergold had met with some "unexpected, uh, complications," and in his place had sent his young relative. Who was trying out this side of the family business as his summer job.

"Not to worry—got the mixin's to mix right here!" Dortmund assured us, popping gum, once he stepped inside. He brought out two packets from his pocket and waggled them in the air. "One's somethin', and the other's—somethin' else! I always get confused!" He scratched his head and grinned. "Hey, what the heck, we'll find out, huh?"

My uncle and I looked at each other in shock.

At this point we heard *"Yoo-hoo!"* from outside

the door. A female voice purred my uncle's name. We all peered out the front window. But it wasn't Linda Cooch standing there underdressed with a huge bouquet of roses and red eyes.

"By the cross-breezes of old Havana," sputtered Uncle Dudley. "Just as I feared—it's the *violinist* from the musicale! I shook her hand too!"

"Wow, she's some tomato!" declared Dortmund Feathergold.

We all went over to the stairs to discuss what to do. My uncle was very concerned; what would happen if Linda Cooch arrived and found competition? "So what's the prob, ya old goat?" wisecracked Dortmund. He clearly had a different view of things.

My uncle's fears were answered by the sudden snarling of female voices from the porch, then the thumping sounds of a struggle. We ran back to the window. "Wowee," cried Dortmund. "Lookit that blondie! She's even *more* tomato!"

His tone suddenly infuriated me.

The violinist got loose from Linda Cooch and ran around toward the rear of the house. My cello

teacher gave chase. Her golden hair was all tangled
and yanked. I gaped.

"Where's yer subscriber stuff?" cried Dortmund. "I'll go mix somethin' for 'em right away!"
There was a treacherous gleam in his eye.

Uncle Dudley stammered that everything was
up on the third floor, but—

Dortmund headed for the stairs without waiting for him to finish.

"But I'm not quite sure you should venture up there!" called Uncle Dudley, following. "I mean, are you entirely qualified for the great task?"

"Hey, what's the big deal?" Dortmund grinned back. He was about to turn off onto the second floor. "Just mix away till ya get it right!"

My uncle protested, then rushed off through the kitchen, to see about the commotion in the backyard. The violinist and Linda Cooch were now struggling and screaming under the maple tree. Slipper, the spaniel, yipped frantically from next door, alone on guard for the evening.

I limped up after Dortmund and found him roaming about, searching for the third-floor stairs. "Where's it?" he demanded.

"My uncle said you really shouldn't go up," I informed him, still simmering over his remark about Linda Cooch.

"Listen, pipsqueak, your nutty uncle is all square in the head," he snorted. "Whatever these tomatoes are on, they need more! So mind your biz, little wiz—here it is!"

He gave me a sneering grin, and disappeared up toward the guest room.

I heard more commotion in the backyard. From the hall window I saw my uncle standing just outside the back door, pleading with both musicians to mind the maple branches. They had joined forces to serenade him from up the tree.

Other voices suddenly drowned them out.

Into the dim yard next door, Stu Bunkmeier and Mr. Feeley came dancing bizarrely, still full of Metamorphic Compound, in their top hats and cloaks. Their eyes glowed, red and creepy. Slipper yapped between them as they sang:

"We're such a naughty twosome,
our intentions are so gruesome!
'Cause we'll paint a naughty poem
that you'll read when you get ho-em!
—and you'll cry!"

They shrieked with laughter, prancing and holding hands. Stu Bunkmeier still had his limp. Neighbors voices began to shout all along Clover Crescent.

Then they started tearing up the flower beds, but I didn't see this because I wasn't watching. I'd heard Dortmund coming back down. He hurried out onto the second floor, chuckling over a vial in his hands. "This'll make 'em merry, oh yessir!" he chuckled. So he wasn't looking up, when I stepped out with a flowerpot, and threw it with all my might on his foot. He screeched—the vial went flying into the wall.

I'd never attacked anyone that much older and bigger before. I limped away fast as I could down the main stairs.

But my ankle gave out by the bottom and I fell, so I was an easy target for Dortmund as he came hopping furiously after me. We rolled around, and he might really have choked me to death—had not Uncle Dudley roared, "Nefarious hooligan!" and thrown himself on Dortmund, not stopping to clean off the lipstick on his goatee and his Panama hat.

So there were the three of us rolling around on the front-hall carpet when the front door suddenly burst open, and a voice I hadn't heard for a while cried:

"*GOD IN HEAVEN HELP US, WHAT IS GOING ON?!*"

And the wail of police sirens drew closer in the night.

CHAPTER TWELVE
voyages resumed

Floating Arthur had stopped floating that morning. He'd landed on a farm a hundred miles away. His parents, the Shetlocks, had gone to fetch him. His strange story—a dazed kid found stuck headfirst in a manure pile—had been broadcast on the radio. My parents, on the last part of their road trip, had heard the broadcast. Right away they phoned Mr. Feeley, who had sounded very very strange. So they drove straight home as fast as they could.

The police now talked with my father, and after giving out lots of tickets for disturbing the

peace (and shushing the reporter from the *Geranium Gazette* off private property), they drove Stu Bunkmeier home to Dot, still in his top hat. She just chuckled. They escorted Mr. Feeley, in his cloak and top hat, back to his deaf elderly mother whom he lived with (I don't think she chuckled). The police told both men to "sleep it off." And they chuckled (the police, I mean).

My father telephoned the college about Linda Cooch and the violinist. They were wrapped in blankets and given a pill to make them sleep. And kept for a long rest at the college clinic.

As for me, my parents drove me for the second night in a row to the Florence Nightingale Hospital emergency room, to have my retwisted ankle rewrapped, and my goose eggs reexamined.

"And now it's time for your uncle to account for himself," announced my father grimly, as we scraped back into our driveway in the green Dodge. *"If he can!"*

But Uncle Dudley wasn't there. And the third-floor guest room was empty, except for a few bare colored boxes. I guess Mr. Adamzicki's station

wagon had been fixed and was available for loading up in a hurry.

Dortmund Feathergold was, of course, long gone—back to East Brooklyn.

"We should *never* have left Duncan like that!" said my mother. "You poor darling. Will you forgive us?" Then she smiled brightly. "Did you get the chili-chocolate sauce we sent?"

Somehow my father survived the article and accompanying photo that came out in the *Gazette*.

For two whole weeks afterward, Arthur could only talk to visitors from his porch, the smell was so bad. He tried to live off his floating adventure when school started in September. But he was dogged forever by how the adventure had ended. Our Gumberry Salvage partnership drifted apart. And then the Shetlocks moved away.

Stu Bunkmeier became his old self again, which was too bad, Dot declared, with a laugh. Mr. Feeley went back to being just Mr. Feeley. Whenever I passed his hedge, though, he'd go a little red and nod, and clear his throat, and stare off somewhere else.

I had one final music lesson, a month later. I stammered to Linda Cooch that I was giving up the cello (Aunt Mac or no Aunt Mac). This was just after she had just informed me that she was quitting teaching; in fact, she was quitting college. She'd be working for the *Geranium Gazette,* where her new fiancé was a rising young reporter. She looked different and relaxed, with her hair in a scarf. She didn't giggle. She said she wanted to introduce me to someone who was just as good a teacher as she was. I gulped and told her my own plans to quit. She just smiled then, and nodded, and said quietly that it was too bad; I had real talent. Can you believe it? And then she put her hand on my arm and gave a squeeze, and another smile—the just-between-us type.

What happened to Aunt Mac's cello on my way out is best forgotten.

More and more I started hanging out at The Reader's Friend bookshop with Mr. Adamzicki. He also took me fishing with him. He fishes the same way he drives. So we've had lots of time to talk about Uncle Dudley and laugh about our amazing summer. Sometimes Mr. Adamzicki and I go to lunch at Kefauver's too. For a while Dot would ask about my uncle, at least at first. Mr. Adamzicki puffs his pipe and tells me always how he can appreciate Uncle Dudley's special respect for Dot, yes he can. I don't say anything.

I started working part-time at the bookshop right before last Christmas. My parents thought it was a great idea after the "bad influence" of Uncle Dudley. And it was Mr. Adamzicki who encouraged me to write.

"You are like your uncle," he said to me. "Maybe a little more sensible, uh? Just a little, I think? And you were shy, but not so shy now? So scribble down what your head sees, and saw, out in the big, funny universe—or deep inside your own starry self."

He gives pretty good advice, I think, Mr. Adamzicki.

As for Uncle Dudley, he's never been back to Mt. Geranium, as you probably guessed. He isn't Mr. Popularity on Clover Crescent as far as my

parents are concerned. "Some *in loco parentis*," my
father still mutters. "God in heaven help us!"

But my uncle writes to me, addressing his
letters in care of Mr. Adamzicki. As you'd expect,
these letters boast faraway return addresses,
though sometimes the *postmark* on them isn't so
exotic at all—a lot more ho-hum. As perhaps by
now you'd also expect.

But they're great letters, full of Uncle
Dudley's marvelous spirit and Knichtbubel
research schemes. Whatever happens, my uncle
never gives up being wizardly in his unique and

curious way. Which was why he was put on this earth, I realize. How could I ever hold my goose eggs against him?

Eventually I hope he'll maybe even sponsor me as a fellow subscriber to the Knichtbubel newsletter. So I can try my own hand—properly—at mastering the challenging researches of the great Feathergold (the uncle, not the grandnephew). Of course I'll probably still have the old Dudley/Duncan luck. I can imagine my left leg disappearing for days, say, before I'm able to summon it back! But I'll keep at it.

What else can I tell you?

Oh, Mr. Adamzicki gave me a secret Christmas gift from Uncle Dudley—something precious of his that he wanted me to have, he said. And it's practically my favorite possession in the world. The shrunken head of Señor Recuerdo, from Mexico! I keep it safe under some socks in my closet, so no one can see it by accident and have a bad shock. I take it out sometimes, when I want a creepy thrill, to recall scary times.

And finally, guess what? I actually received a letter from Hettie Buckle, back at the end of that magical summer! My mother found it by the maple tree:

Oh Yung Kyne Surr!

Oh Pleyse to ixkews oor dredful kertisy at Famer Swinsin fild, Abe Basket iz a onest mun, he is mos sory & ashayme, he pledds yr kindnis. Mysef tew. We arr viktims of demin mylk. Wer kan we get more of that ondirfil choklit sorce? It waz sew gud!

Wyth honis harte,
Hettie Buckle (hrselff)

When the new jar that we ordered arrived from Cincinnati, Mr. Adamzicki and I left it under the moon in Farmer Swenson's field. But, of course, we didn't stay to watch the goblins eat it.

Acknowledgments

My heartfelt thanks—seven of the Sultan's treasure-chests' worth—to Douglas Gayeton, Mark Richard, Knight Landesman, Tom Schnabel, Juliet Bashore, Aaron Slavin, and my brothers Palle and Tug. Same to Jill Grinberg, for the inspiration to write for children and for nursing early versions along; and to the marvelous team at Candlewick, particularly my incisive and subtle editor, Deborah Wayshak, for keeping at it until they got my best from me. Appreciations of another kind to Northampton, Massachusetts, for favorite memories of where I was a kid. And to Anya von Bremzen . . . for pretty much everything.